THE FRENCH ART
OF STEALING

THE FRENCH ART
OF STEALING

a novel by
Mark Beauregard

A GIANT BOOK

Second Giant Publishing Edition January 2019

Bibliographical Note: This novel is an unabridged reprint of the same novel published in 2006 under the name Mark Zero. Mark Zero and Mark Beauregard are both pen names of Beauregard Mark Zero. First Giant Publishing Edition December 2006.

Library of Congress Control Number: 2019932907

ISBN: 978-1-933975-09-2

10 9 8 7 6 5 4 3 2 1

Cover Images: Comstock Images
Author Photograph: © 2005 Rose Todaro

www.giantpublishing.com

CONTENTS

1

Le Marais

People shoot at me all the time, but it's nothing personal. I'm a photojournalist—a war photographer, to be precise. I risk my neck so that you can calmly survey scenes of violence half a world away as you sip your morning coffee. I've been attacked with rocket-propelled grenades in the jungles of Côte d'Ivoire, held at knife-point in a collapsed mosque in Fallujah, hit by a jeep during a firefight outside of Medellin. The chance of death is both the price and the perverse attraction of the job, and it's compensated by a freedom that most people rarely enjoy—as an experienced freelancer, I work when and if I want, travel to the most exotic places imaginable, and require only the hatred of man for his fellow man to keep my creditors at bay.

Bullets have been whizzing past my ears for so long that I don't usually tell stories about them any more, but in this case an exception is in order: the bullet that ricocheted off the stones of the Pont Neuf a few inches from my head was different from the others. No war was raging in downtown Paris that night, no revolutionaries were trying to capture the Île de la Cité. That bullet was meant for me, personally, and when I jumped off the bridge into the Seine, the bullets that followed me into the river were meant for me as well. Fortunately, the shooter was as unfamiliar with guns as I was with fine art, and he was probably just as surprised to be shooting at me as I was to have his priceless painting, a masterpiece by the Post-Impressionist Maximilien Luce.

How I came to have the painting is a relatively simple tale;

what happened after I got it is a little more complicated, so it may be best to begin at the beginning, on a warm summer evening in the section of Paris's Right Bank known as the Marais.

* * * * *

Marais means swamp in French and the name couldn't be more apt. Originally an actual swamp before the land was drained in the thirteenth century, the Marais is now a metropolitan muck and muddle, dirty, rich and teeming with life. The streets are narrow, the buildings high and grimy, and though the prospect of a chivalrous death is now remote, the architecture still suggests *The Three Musketeers*. Kings and counts built palaces here; the palaces still stand, but they've been sectioned up and are now occupied by haute couture boutiques fighting for space with tobacco shops and seedy pawnbrokers. On a given day in the Marais, you can see fashion models elbowing street hustlers for room on the tiny slivers of sidewalks, both heading for the same centuries-old but newly trendy cafe.

I moved into the Marais ten years ago, when I needed a European home base while working for the New York *Times*. The fallen grandeur and grungy beauty suit me. There are always crowds on the street, day and night, and the anonymity of such a constant press of people soothes my soul. After weeks in Central African villages, it's a relief to see only casual disdain in others' eyes, rather than suspicion or pure hatred. There is rarely any real violence here, just constant uproar, yelling and theatrical bickering, accompanied by the smell of fresh-baked baguettes wafting from every corner bakery.

The evening I became an international art thief, the electricity in my apartment had cut out, thanks to some incompetent carpenters who were remodeling a shop in the next building. This meant that my tiny window fan could no longer offer its meager defense against the sweltering July heat, so I walked down the five flights to the street. The sun was still high at seven in the evening and the people on the street looked drained and sullen, their hair and clothes limp with sweat and humidity. I glared at the hapless carpenters, who were too busy yelling at each other to notice me.

I strolled around the corner to the little fruit market on rue des Tournelles. Plump cherries, peaches and watermelons spilled artfully across the wooden tables that blocked the sidewalk on either side of the door. I called in to Etienne, the owner.

"*Salut*, Luke," Etienne said, stepping out onto the street, wiping his big, hairy-knuckled hands on his apron. Etienne's family had owned this fruit market for three generations, since they had moved here from Algiers, but his son had married a Swiss woman and moved to Zurich and his daughter was studying to be a lawyer: no one would carry on the tradition, and when Etienne retired this little space would become a fashionable hair salon or a designer lingerie boutique. Like all the old immigrant markets in the Marais, Etienne's *fruiterie* would eventually become a high-end bauble shop.

I bought an apricot. "You see the protest at the Place des Vosges this morning?"

Just around the corner from Etienne's market, Louis XIII had once hosted jousting tournaments at the Place des Vosges. Now buskers sang for coins there and souvenir stands offered tourists gaudy little pieces of Paris.

Etienne dismissed the protest with a wave of his hand. "Stupid students! Who cares if they make a national identity card? The government knows all it wants to know about us already. That's what governments do, they keep track of you. You can't hide from the government."

"You don't believe in the right to privacy?"

"Sure. I believe in the right to own cats on the moon, too. That doesn't mean there are cats on the moon."

I patted Etienne's shoulder and wished him a *bonne soirée*. He continued this conversation with another customer.

I ate the apricot as I threaded my way through a crush of people toward L'Elephant Heureux, "the Happy Elephant." That's my neighborhood watering hole, where I spend almost every evening I'm in Paris. I usually show up close to midnight, but this seemed like a good day to start early on Pelforth blondes and armagnac.

When I arrived, Benoît was already there, the only customer, sitting at the end of the bar wearing the light green coveralls issued to him by the City of Paris. He was waving his arms, making animated declarations to the Elephant's owner, Jean-Pierre. Jean-Pierre was, customarily, inhaling a Gitane. He blew gray smoke and nodded hello.

"If it's in the river," Benoît was saying, "then it's part of the river. There's no difference between the river and what's in it."

Jean-Pierre stroked his thick, curly gray beard philosophically. "A fish is not a river. A boat is not a river. If I throw a cigarette into the river, the butt is not the river."

"You can't talk about the spine and not mention the nerve endings," Benoît countered. "You can't separate the water from what it carries. It's a *system*." He said this as if it were a triumph of Socratic logic.

I sat down next to him and indicated the Pelforth tap with a nod and a glance. Jean-Pierre slid down the bar and poured me a beer.

I had known Jean-Pierre since his days as a board operator at Radio France. He had always dreamed of owning a bar, and after twenty years of hustle and headaches in broadcasting, he had finally saved enough money to open the Elephant. That was seven years ago, and his pace had slowed every year

4

since. In fact, he had become like a happy elephant himself, moving deliberately, with a bulky, fluid grace that hid a slow and rarely aroused temper. He liked to say that opening the Elephant had finally given him time to smoke properly, and he attracted regulars who resembled him, in having a great capacity for industry but preferring indolence.

"Did you see *Le Monde* today?" Jean-Pierre asked as he set my beer in front of me.

"About the Seine?"

"What you have to question," Benoît said, "is who asked for that study and why? Who will use it and for what reason?"

A new study about the noxious filth in the Seine had appeared in that morning's paper, and Benoît was predictably offended. Benoît loved the river. As an unemployed garbage collector, he had lots of time on his hands, and he dedicated it to the Seine, though even he could not say why. He would only shrug his shoulders and say "*Je l'aime.*" He read books about the river, hitched rides up and down it on coal barges, drank by it, slept by it and threw up into its sludgy green waters. He had become so obsessed with the Seine that he threw himself off the Pont Marie every Friday night and then swam downstream, sometimes as far as the Eiffel Tower. It was a baptism and a communion at once, an almost religious offering of himself to the river. It was also a slow and phlegmatic way of committing suicide in the bacteriological stew of the water—and it would be a slow suicide only if a barge or tourist boat didn't accidentally run him down one night.

"Quite an industrial cocktail," I said. The study had found levels of mercury over 100 times higher than normal in the Seine, along with cadmium, lead, chromium and other toxic killers. "I'm surprised it hasn't congealed into a neon green pudding."

Benoît scoffed. "The studies are all correct, of course," he said angrily, "but no one knows what they mean. No one can interpret them. You have to ask the river what they mean."

I exchanged a look with Jean-Pierre, who took a long drag on his cigarette and squinted through the smoke. "What do *you* think they mean?"

Benoît thought for a moment. "The Seine is France's digestive tract. It brings us our food and carries away our shit. If our digestive tract is toxic, then the disease is in us, not outside of us. We need to heal ourselves."

He drained off his whiskey and set it down on the bar. Jean-Pierre refilled it and poured himself one as well. It looked like it was going to be just another Thursday at the Happy Elephant, and I took a deep drink of my beer, thinking it was about time I found another war to visit. That's when Giselle's red BMW Z8 came screaming to a stop on the street outside.

Giselle is an antique dealer, with a high-ticket shop that she inherited from her mother. She has short blonde hair, icy blue eyes, and a brusque, offhanded manner, and she knows the value of things in eight different currencies. She usually moves like a metronome, with precise steps and compact gestures, which was why it surprised me to see her fishtail her tiny sports car to a stop in the middle of rue des Tournelles, fling herself out the driver's door and lurch toward the Happy Elephant. Her ankle-length skirt bunched unattractively as she fought against it for speed. Then I realized it wasn't the skirt that was making her stumble along so awkwardly: she was limping, as if she had sprained an ankle. Her car was blocking traffic, and honking horns and angry shouts followed her into the bar.

Her eyes darted from Jean-Pierre to Benoît before settling on me. "Luke, thank God you're here." She hobbled quickly toward the back of the room. "Follow me," she called over her shoulder, and then she disappeared into the bathroom.

I hesitated.

"Luke!" Giselle screamed, sticking her head out of the water closet. "Now!"

Jean-Pierre ushered me toward her with both hands, a look of confusion and urgency in his eyes. I jumped up and ran.

Like many small bars in Paris, the Elephant has just one tiny restroom for both men and women, and though I knew Giselle well, she had never invited me to go to the toilet with her. I hesitated again at the bathroom door and glanced outside, where a crowd was beginning to clot the street around Giselle's car.

Giselle grabbed me by the shirt and pulled me in after her. I nearly toppled into the toilet bowl. She spun around to face me and I grabbed onto her shoulders to regain my balance.

Her shirt was soaked through with sweat, and I could smell panic and perfume mixing on her neck and arms. Her eyes were wide and determined, and as I opened my mouth to ask what on earth was going on, she began unfastening her belt.

"Listen to me," she said, slipping out of her skirt. "I'm going to give you something, and you have to promise you'll keep it for me, just for tonight." She quickly and carefully turned her skirt inside out, and I saw why it had looked so strange, why she had run so awkwardly into the bar: she had used hairpins to clip a canvas to the underneath side. She unclipped it, turned the painted side of the canvas toward me and shoved it into my hands. "I stole this—but it's all right, it doesn't belong to the people I stole it from. I'll explain later. Just stay here at the Elephant until closing time, then find some way to get it home without anyone seeing you. I'll call you at your apartment just after two o'clock."

"You *stole* this?"

She stepped back into her skirt. "If anyone follows me here, I had to use the bathroom, I used the bathroom, then I ran out again, all right? You didn't follow me into the toilet, there was no painting, that's all you know. I ran in, I ran out. And for God's sake, keep the painting hidden!"

"But—"

"I can count on you, can't I?" She buckled her belt and then kissed me on the cheek. "Thanks a million, Luke." She turned and unlocked the bathroom door all in one blurry motion and bolted out. "It's not how it looks," she called, as she ran for the Elephant's front door.

I peeked out of the bathroom to see Giselle fighting her way through the crowd of onlookers to her BMW. Cursing from the cars stranded behind her serenaded her into the driver's seat, and I took the opportunity, while everyone outside focused on Giselle's sudden reappearance, to slip out of the toilet with the painting and dart behind the bar. Giselle slammed her car door, hit the gas and raced off down the street.

I squeezed around Jean-Pierre and knelt to open the trap door into his wine cellar. "Be careful," Jean-Pierre said quietly. "Lightswitch is on your left at the bottom." This was an extraordinary concession, since the one cardinal rule of the Elephant was that no one but Jean-Pierre was allowed behind the bar, much less in the cellar.

I struggled down the metal steps, felt around for the lightswitch, and found myself staring into a bare bulb that hung just at eye level. I blinked hard into the cellar until the shapes of boxes and wine racks fixed themselves all around me. Calling this space a cellar, it turned out, was overstating the matter considerably: I was in a six-by-four room, barely tall enough for me to stand upright, crammed floor to ceiling with cases of alcohol.

The canvas Giselle had given me was about three feet long

and two feet tall, a rectangle too big to fit neatly inside a wine case. I scooted some boxes of bordeaux away from the wall, slipped the painting behind them to the floor, and then pushed the boxes back against it.

Satisfied, I wiped my hands and turned to climb back up the ladder, when I heard Jean-Pierre hiss, "Turn out the light." He slammed the trap door in my face and I heard the latch click shut from the outside. I turned out the light.

Beads of sweat appeared on my upper lip. When I found that I was unconsciously panting, I held my breath. I was trapped in a tiny wine cellar with a stolen painting, and something unpleasant was going on in the bar above me.

It would not be just another Thursday at the Happy Elephant.

2

Maximilien Luce

I remember once in Monrovia, Liberia, during one of the many insurgencies or counterinsurgencies in that country's short history, I found myself trapped in the walk-in refrigerator of a restaurant that was suddenly the scene of a firefight. Only stupidity or fate or a combination of the two might persuade a person to take shelter from a gun battle in a refrigerator, but that's what we did.

There were three of us jammed into the tight little space: the reporter I was accompanying, a local guide and me. After half a minute of constant machine gun fire, followed by three minutes of more sporadic shooting and then a few more minutes of silence, our guide believed that the fight had moved to another venue. Over my objection, he opened the refrigerator door and motioned for us to follow him out. I shook my head emphatically no, but the guide continued out into the kitchen. I grabbed the reporter's wrist, shook my head no again and quietly pulled the refrigerator door closed.

Not fifteen seconds later, we heard gunfire. We would later discover our guide's body in the dining area. Why no one bothered to come into the kitchen and kill us I don't know, but we stayed in that refrigerator until our teeth chattered, and then we stayed a little longer—the glamorous life of a war photographer.

I thought about that long-ago moment as I crouched in the dark cellar beneath the Happy Elephant. This little dilemma was nothing by comparison—no one would burst into the bar with machine guns blazing, no one would drag me out of the cellar and beat my head into pulp. This was just the Marais. Whatever was happening would not end in anyone's death—at least, I didn't think so at the time.

I heard Jean-Pierre's footfalls overhead as he walked to the other end of the bar. He stopped, and then I heard muffled male voices, an exchange between Jean-Pierre and someone new, but it was impossible to tell what was going on.

Giselle had said that she'd stolen the painting but not from its rightful owners, so whoever was speaking to Jean-Pierre was either the original thief, the rightful owner or the police, and I couldn't decide who I'd rather have catch me with it. I supposed hiding the painting at all, in however amateurish a fashion, still made me an accessory to the crime, but I wasn't even sure what the crime was.

It seemed so unreal that I hardly even believed it was happening, especially since it involved Giselle. You might never meet a more sensible, forthright and honorable person than Giselle, and I could not imagine the circumstances that would lead her to steal a cocktail napkin, much less a valuable painting. More than that, she'd had no qualms about making me her accomplice, and I couldn't believe she would voluntarily put any of her friends in harm's way. Something else was going on, something that made some kind of sense, but the only clear thing at that moment was that I trusted Giselle enough to wait for the explanation.

As seconds turned to minutes and minutes started to feel like hours, I felt more and more that something truly dangerous might be happening, though it was happening for the moment without me. I wondered if Giselle might be in real peril. I wondered if I was.

After a long time standing braced for action, I was finally overcome by the heat and felt around for a sturdy box to sit on.

I mopped my brow and waited for Jean-Pierre to come get me, or for the police to haul me out and handcuff me, or for God-knew-who to come down looking for a fight.

* * * * *

The first time I met Jean-Pierre was at a Press Club event at the Tour d'Argent, an insanely expensive restaurant on the Left Bank. Most of the writers and editors gathered on that special occasion could not have afforded an aperitif there, much less the five-course dinner they served us, so everyone was having the time of their lives. Me, I hate pretentious restaurants and starched linens; I feel more comfortable with eccentrics and revolutionaries, and too much respectable company eventually makes me nervous. After gulping down a few glasses of Billecart Salmon Brut, I escaped to the restroom feeling harassed and found Jean-Pierre there, wearing exactly the same beleaguered expression I was.

"Fucking tuxedos," he said, by way of introduction. We formed an instant bond.

In the years that followed, I would see that expression on his face often as he navigated the political world of broadcast journalism—an expression of sublimated fear and exasperation. He hated the way even well-intentioned media shaped and biased the news, and he hated dealing with the unappeasable egos of the broadcasters. Since he had founded the Happy Elephant, that fearful, exasperated expression had disappeared, but when he finally opened his wine cellar to let me out that night—four hours after he'd locked me in—he was wearing it again.

"What the hell has been going on?" I said, as I climbed up the ladder. I was soaked in my own sweat, and Jean-Pierre gave me a towel to wipe myself off.

Benoît was still there, sitting now in one of the easy chairs across the room, obviously extremely drunk. Half a dozen other regulars were scattered around the bar, a tiny crowd for a Thursday night at the Happy Elephant. The dim wall lamps were on, the usual Latin jazz played softly on the sound system, and cigarette smoke curled through the air—everything looked normal, but the atmosphere in the place was charged and uncertain. I glanced out toward the street, which was now dark and offered no clues about what had happened.

"Hey, Jean-Pierre," Heloise called. Heloise owned a spice shop down the street. "How does Luke suddenly rate—?"

It was supposed to be a jocular comment on the fact that I had entered the forbidden territory behind the bar, but her tone was forced, and the joke stopped abruptly before it had ended, as Heloise realized that I had not rounded the bar but instead emerged from underneath it. A pall was hanging over the room anyway, and my curious emergence only added to the strangeness. Everyone looked from Jean-Pierre to me for an explanation.

"Who came in before?" I whispered.

"A couple of assholes, chasing Giselle," he breathed. "Looked like tough customers. One of them took off right away, the other stayed behind. He only just left."

"And Giselle?"

Jean-Pierre indicated that he had not heard from her. "What did she give you?"

"Didn't you see it? A painting. It's behind the bordeaux."

"Which bordeaux?"

"I don't know. Chateau Something-or-other."

Jean-Pierre rolled his eyes.

Though this entire conversation was taking place *sotto voce*, it was dominating the bar. Everyone was looking to us for some clue about the weirdness they were feeling, about the identity of the menacing stranger who had just left, about why I had been in the cellar all evening. As our lips moved theatrically without sound, all other conversations stopped.

"Come on," I said. "Let's go up to your rooms."

"No. I believe the bar is being watched." In order to get to Jean-Pierre's apartment above the Elephant, you had to step out onto the street and enter the building through a separate doorway. "It might be better to stay in a more public place."

"So you're going to sleep in the bar tonight?" If someone was waiting and watching outside, I wondered how I would ever make it home—three blocks away—with the painting.

"I'm tempted to call the police," Jean-Pierre said. "I don't need this kind of trouble, but the police might be bad for Giselle."

"Well, we can't stay here for the rest of our lives. At least, I can't."

Giselle had said she would call me at my apartment at two o'clock. As long as Jean-Pierre and a few patrons remained at the Elephant, I figured it would be safe to leave the painting in the cellar, at least until last call. That would give me just under three hours to go home, make some phone calls and try to find out what the hell was going on. And even if some thug stopped me on the street, he wouldn't find the painting on me and he could hardly just beat me up, not with the sizable bar crowd still milling from club to club in the Marais. This wasn't New York or Mexico City.

I told Jean-Pierre my intentions and then realized that I hadn't taken a good look at the painting, and that I couldn't learn anything about it if I didn't even know what it was. Cursing my thoughtlessness, I opened the trap door and slipped back down the ladder. There could now be no doubt to anyone watching that the cellar was the center of the drama.

I flipped on the light, retrieved the canvas from behind the boxes of bordeaux and held it up to the bare bulb. I suddenly wished I'd gone to any of the ten thousand museums in Paris, even once.

As a journalist, I had always been more interested in the Spanish Civil War photographs of Robert Capa than in Goya's etchings of those same battles. When I needed romance, I turned to Robert Doisneau's warm black-and-white photos of couples kissing in the rain rather than the blurry pink pastels of Claude Monet's garden paintings. I had once seen a Monet exhibit at the MOMA in New York, and after viewing the hundredth soft blue painting of the Thames in a row, I had left in disgust.

The canvas now in my hands was an oil painting, a colorful river scene somewhere out in the country, with a pink and blue sky and bolder greens, yellows, reds and purples representing grasses and wildflowers along the river's banks. There were no boats or people or animals, just a peaceful landscape. It was painted in an interesting style, without brushstrokes; instead, there were hundreds of little dots of paint. The closer you came to the painting, the more it seemed like a random collection of dots, and the farther away you got, the more it coalesced into a unified picture. The artist's signature was at the bottom right: Maximilien Luce. I had never heard of him.

I slid the canvas back into its hiding place and climbed back up. A few more people had just staggered in, some drunks who had started drinking somewhere else, and they shouted a rousing welcome when they saw me appear from under the bar. Nothing like a gaggle of drunks to restore order—the Elephant was feeling more and more like its normal self.

I told Jean-Pierre I would phone him an hour before closing. Then I gave him a significant look that I hoped he would interpret as, "Guard that painting like a fifty-year-old bottle of calvados."

Out on the street, I joined the crowds of people flowing up rue des Tournelles. As usual, Germans, Spaniards, Americans, Japanese and who-knew how many others were talking amongst themselves in their own languages, or pidgin versions of someone else's language, creating a rowdy babble of semi-sensible noise. There were enough people around that, if someone had been watching and following me, he could have blended in undetectably. I tried not to think about it and marched home.

I saw lights on in some of the windows in my building—thankfully, the electricity had been restored. At the outside door, I punched a four-digit code into the electronic keypad, and the lock on the door clicked open. I stepped into the tiny, narrow passageway and waited for the outside door to close; then I quickly punched a second four-digit code into the inner keypad, and the door to the main stairwell clicked open. I entered and waited for the second door to lock as well and then climbed the stairs to my one-room apartment. For the moment, I was safe.

I dialed Giselle's cell phone number, which shunted me immediately to her voice mail. I called her home, got her answering machine and thought better of leaving a message. Giselle was indisposed.

I booted up my computer and logged onto the internet. A search for Maximilien Luce quickly led me to several sites about Impressionists, Post-Impressionists and Pointillists, and I found a page with digital reproductions of some of Luce's paintings. One of them, *La Seine à Herblay*, dated 1890, looked strikingly like the one in Jean-Pierre's cellar. The perspective was not quite the same, and I thought there might be a series of such canvases, the way Monet had painted the same scene over and over again from different angles, in different lights. Herblay was a small town in Normandy, downstream from Paris, and I thought how happy Benoît would be when he found out that all the fuss was over a painting of the Seine.

I printed out a short biography of Luce and then shut off the computer. It was just after midnight.

I phoned Jean-Pierre, who reported that no more menacing strangers had appeared, Giselle had not returned, and the Elephant was to all appearances back to its normal self. When I told him he had a Post-Impressionist masterpiece hidden under his feet, he said, "*Tu blagues*! We'll all go to prison!"

"Just sit tight. We'll wait for Giselle to call, and if I don't hear from her by two-thirty, we'll phone the police. You'll know when I know."

I hung up, boiled water for coffee and had just sat down to read the biography of Maximilien Luce when my doorbell rang. I leapt up and went to the door.

It couldn't be the landlady, not at midnight; my girlfriend Séverine was still at work, preparing for the fashion show. It hardly seemed possible that one of the toughs from the Elephant had followed me home, copped my security codes without my seeing him and then managed to locate my exact studio in a sprawling seven-story apartment building. My windows don't even open onto the street, but rather into the building's inner courtyard, so no one would have seen my lights come on even if they *had* followed me home. And whoever was following Giselle couldn't possibly know who I was. Or could they?

The bell rang again. "Who's there?" I called. "Giselle?"

The doorbell insisted. Then I heard a body lean heavily into my door and a single knock came, up high, as if someone's head had banged against it. The wooden floorboards in the hall creaked heavily, and a body slid slowly to the floor. I could hear fingers scraping all the way down the door.

"Giselle?" I unbolted the lock and swung the door in.

Because I was looking down when I stepped into the hall,

I did not get a good look at the object that slammed into the top of my head. I saw a man in a blue suit lying prone in my hallway, grinning up at me. I saw the red dungarees and white t-shirt of his upright partner, who clocked me. I felt an instant of shock, and then pain, and then I crashed down on top of the grinning ogre in the blue suit.

3

Benoît Takes The Painting

You may wonder how a person who demonstrates such poor judgment could have survived twenty years as a war photographer. There are two reasons: the first is that I'm lucky, though I did not feel lucky when I woke up in my apartment. I felt stupid—but then, there's a reason we call luck dumb.

The second reason is that I tend to defy people's expectations. People—violent revolutionaries included—expect each other to behave with some predictability, even in the most chaotic situations; if someone does something outlandish, everyone may suddenly act less coherently. Many times I have seen seemingly impossible maneuvers and half-baked ploys actually succeed, because, in the split second when choices are made, in the instant when everyone must react, one incongruous move can lead to a whole series of improbable acts, and people may then fail to heed their own best interests.

I read a story once about football great Walter Payton—it said that he always had his best games against the best defenses, because they were disciplined and always in the right position. Since Payton knew where the defensive players were supposed to be all over the field, he knew where the holes would be and he would sprint through them. With sloppy defenses, he never knew where anyone might be at any given moment, and he sometimes gave his worst performances against the worst teams. I am like the bad defense that somehow manages to baffle the best offensive backs.

I awoke slowly, with a harsh ringing in my ears and an

early morning sun shining through my window. I propped myself up on one elbow. Someone had thoughtfully deposited me in my bed and then ransacked my apartment. The ringing in my ears continued intermittently, until I realized it was my doorbell.

My head seemed twice its normal size. I touched the spot where I had been sapped and felt a sharp pain but no matted blood. "*Merde*," I muttered to the sunshine. I dragged myself out of bed and stumbled to the door.

All my books were scattered across the floor, my posters and pictures ripped from their frames and my furniture dragged away from the walls. The cushions of my chairs had been slashed open. I glanced into the tiny kitchen and saw that the cupboards had been emptied.

Still, they hadn't smashed my computer or ripped the phone from the wall or beaten me gratuitously. They had been looking for the painting, and when they hadn't found it, they'd left. Perhaps polite was not the best word to describe them, but if this had happened in Guatemala, those goons would certainly have destroyed everything and killed me just for sport. Thank God I live in a civil society.

The doorbell rang again and Séverine called my name. I opened the door and ushered her in. The shock on her face when she saw me was gratifying, and I gladly melted into her embrace. She guided me back into bed, where she cooed and stroked my face and expressed her outrage and bewilderment at the state of my apartment.

Séverine is a *chapelière*, a hat-maker, and has been my lover on and off for nearly eight years. She has lustrous, curly black hair and dark almond eyes. She owns a little shop on rue des Franc-Bourgeois, one of the main shopping streets in the Marais, where she competes with three other *chapelleries*. Only in Paris could four shops whose only product is haute couture hats survive within a kilometer of each other.

Séverine thrives mainly because she makes hats for many of the international fashion designers who premiere their new clothes in Paris twice a year. She always wears avant-garde fashions, because the designers give her their creations at cost: this morning she was wearing a lime green mini-dress with giant black polka dots and a black hat that looked like it had blown off the pages of *Gone With the Wind*. She held a baguette in her hand.

She took off her hat, laid the baguette across the mess atop my tiny dresser and sat down next to me on the bed. I told her everything that had happened. She kissed my lips, tenderly kissed the knot on top of my head and then went into the kitchen to fill a towel with ice. To a certain extent, Séverine had become accustomed to seeing me injured, nursing me through scrapes large and small whenever I returned from covering a story in the field; she was not, however, used to witnessing the scenes of the injuries.

"So you never heard from Giselle again?" she asked, when I had finished my story.

"I've been unconscious until this moment." I glanced around the room and located the answering machine. Though the goons hadn't broken or disconnected it, its red light was flashing a rapid distress signal: no one could have left a message. When my power had cut out the previous evening, the machine had lost its memory and I hadn't bothered to reset it when I'd come home. I kicked myself for not replacing the back-up battery a month ago.

"I wonder how Jean-Pierre's getting along," I said, as Séverine returned with the ice for my head. I picked up the phone and dialed Jean-Pierre's home number. He answered immediately.

"I thought something terrible had happened to you," he

said.

"It did." I described the attack of the previous evening and then asked what had happened at his place.

"Those guys came back and I called the cops," Jean-Pierre said.

"So that's it, then? The cops have the thugs and the painting?"

"No, the thugs got away, and Benoît has the painting."

"Benoît?"

"He's on a barge somewhere upriver. I'll tell you about it when I see you. When can you meet me at the bar?"

"But what about Giselle? Have you heard from her?"

"No. You mean you haven't either?"

There was a mutual pause pregnant with worry, then we agreed to meet in an hour and hung up. Séverine continued fussing and cooing over my injuries, and I reported that Benoît had the painting on a barge.

"Benoît has a priceless stolen painting? He's likely to trade it for a *Croque-Monsieur*," she said. "How are you feeling?"

"I'd feel better myself after a *Croque-Monsieur*," I said, realizing that I hadn't eaten since lunch the day before.

Séverine offered to make me breakfast before she left to open her shop. Next week was couture week in Paris: the designers were showing their new styles for the upcoming autumn and winter, and Séverine still had a mountain of hats to make for the shows.

"You need to go to the hospital," Séverine told me. "And then you need to go to the police." She knew I would do neither.

She took her baguette into my kitchen and started restoring order. I reset my answering machine and then sorted through my wrecked belongings, making a mental catalog of the damage.

* * * * *

The Happy Elephant's front door was open when I arrived—the panes of its middle two windows were broken out, replaced with cardboard and masking tape, but the bar seemed otherwise unmolested. I stepped inside and found Jean-Pierre sitting on a barstool, drinking the last of an espresso. He offered me one and, as he went behind the bar to make it, he told me what had happened the previous evening.

After he had spoken to me on the phone at midnight, he had decided to close early. He couldn't keep his cool mixing drinks under such duress: he was sure at every moment that the thugs were going to return, and he was worried about Giselle. Jean-Pierre, more than anything, loves peace and harmony—he wants no part of trouble, especially illegal trouble. He announced last call and shut the Elephant's doors at one-thirty in the morning, and then waited with Benoît for either me or Giselle to call. When neither of us did, he began a slow-motion panic, and by two o'clock, when the thugs returned, he was sure we were all in over our heads.

The thugs demanded that he open the door. He refused. They broke in the glass, and while they were fumbling to clear the shards and unlock the door, Jean-Pierre called the police. There is a police station half a kilometer away on rue de Rivoli, and in no time the honking drone of sirens sounded down the street. The thugs fled.

Realizing that Giselle might wind up in jail if he turned the stolen painting over to the *gendarmes*, Jean-Pierre quickly got the canvas from his wine cellar. He had just stuffed it down the back of Benoît's green garbage collector coveralls when the police arrived at his door. Jean-Pierre told them that the miscreants had been there earlier, were probably just out to rob the place, and that he had never seen them before and didn't know why they had chosen his bar. He did not mention me or Giselle or the painting—as much as Jean-Pierre hates trouble, he loves his friends more and will go to great lengths to protect them, including making himself a criminal accessory.

Benoît was still drunk as the police were leaving, and Jean-Pierre persuaded them to give him a lift "home," considering the uncertain circumstances. Benoît gave the address of a quay at the east end of the city, where he knew some of the bargees, and the police escorted him and the painting there, where he could hide it.

"The whole time the police were here," Jean-Pierre said, "Benoît was carrying on drunkenly, making a fool of himself so the policemen would become annoyed with him and stop paying attention. So they wouldn't notice that he had a stolen masterpiece slipping down his back."

"And you haven't heard from Benoît since?"

"No. And I have no idea which *péniche* he was heading for." *Péniche* is a general term used to designate French river barges. Jean-Pierre lit a cigarette and took a long drag as the espresso machine finished steaming out our coffees.

"You think Giselle knows what she's doing?"

Jean-Pierre shrugged. "She always has." He set two cups on the bar and then came around and sat on the stool next to mine. "But then, I've never known her to steal art before."

We sat for a while, stirring and sipping, hoping that Giselle had not run afoul of her pursuers or, for that matter, of the law. I wondered if some slick underworld tough had followed Benoît's police escort down to the river.

"So what now?" Jean-Pierre said, exhaling smoke.

I reached around the bar for the telephone and dialed Giselle's cell number. I got her voice mail, and then I reached her answering machine again at her home number.

"Nothing we can do about Giselle," I said, "unless we go to the police."

Jean-Pierre's eyes were dewey and uncertain. "She could be in real jeopardy, Luke."

"I know. We'll have to report what happened if we don't hear from her soon—but I say we trust her for now. Meantime, I'm going to buy all the morning papers and see if they say anything about it. If that turns up nothing, I'll call the *Herald* and find somebody who might know what's going on. Stolen art usually finds its way into the news, sooner or later. You know anybody likely, somebody on the city beat maybe, or the arts section?"

Jean-Pierre shook his head no. "I've lost touch with that crowd. Besides, I never got along with most of you print guys—you drink too much." His eyes glinted at his own joke.

I stood up to leave. "I've got my cell phone," I said, taking it out of my pocket and holding it up for emphasis. "Call me the instant you hear anything."

Jean-Pierre nodded and told me to take care of myself. I finished my espresso and left the Happy Elephant.

4

Le Musée d'Orsay

As I walked up rue Saint Antoine toward the Place de la Bastille, I dialed the number of the *International Herald-Tribune*. I asked for Jay Cutler, an old crony of mine, was mildly surprised to learn that he was actually in the office so early, and then was put on hold. I remained on hold all the way to the Place de la Bastille, where I stopped at a kiosk and scanned headlines in five different languages. The phone clicked and I was cut off. Typical.

I flipped through a number of newspapers but found nothing at first glance about art thefts, Post-Impressionists or car chases through Paris. Realizing that Giselle must have come across the painting at an estate she was dealing with through her antique shop, I looked at *Le Monde*'s obituaries section for likely candidates; however, someone might be dead an indefinite amount of time before their belongings were parted out to auction houses and antique dealers, and no one of obvious patrician wealth was memorialized today.

I spent fifteen euros buying an armload of major papers, and then dialed Jay again. Once again, I was put on hold and then cut off.

I headed for the metro station near the kiosk. It was a straight shot on the number one line from the Bastille to the west-Paris suburb of Neuilly-sur-Seine, where the *Herald*'s offices were located. If Jay stayed put for just thirty minutes, I could catch him in person.

* * * * *

At rush hour, the Paris metro was a giant seething ant farm of bodies pushing and writhing against each other. The turnstiles into the platforms rotated non-stop with people of all kinds, in all manner of costumes, dodging and passing and stepping over one another in a rush to get to their offices and shops, where they would undoubtedly, after the French tradition, take a twenty minute coffee break. I arrived at the number one platform just as a train pulled up, and I slithered into an already jam-packed car.

For the brief time it took to travel to the next metro stop, there was still enough room to stand without actually touching anyone else; but at Saint-Paul, a gaggle of people got on and nobody got off. A guy in a business suit pressed up against my back. I moved forward to get out of his way, but he pressed against me harder—I believe he did this against his will, but you can never tell on the metro. The knuckles of the hand he was using to hold his briefcase began making an indentation in my posterior.

A sudden jolt of the train as it started again squashed me against the woman facing me. Our bodies were touching along their whole lengths, and I had to turn my head to avoid breathing directly into her ear. I detected that she had washed her hair that morning with an apple essence shampoo, had used an almond skin cream and wore Chanel perfume. Her breasts pressed against my ribs as we raced along. At every curve and jostle of the tracks, my body rubbed against hers, and the fist of the guy behind me edged toward increasingly delicate areas. This went on with progressive intimacy for ten minutes, until I knew every contour of the woman's body and the man's briefcase was between my knees.

Finally, at the second Louvre stop, the crowd cleared out a little. I'd had sex with people I hadn't gotten as close to, but the woman got off the train without even shaking my hand, and the guy with his fist in my derriere didn't even tip me. I reminded myself for the thousandth time never to take the metro at rush hour. I got off five minutes later at the Pont Neuilly stop and rushed with the other worker ants up the steps and out into the sunshine.

Whereas I'd entered the metro in a storied quarter of Paris, where kings had banqueted and the French Revolution had started, I left it in a section of the suburbs so ugly it might just as easily have been Lima, Peru. Neuilly occupies a stretch of land just north of the Bois de Boulogne and just west of the Arc de Triomphe. Its civic buildings are primarily recent, dating from the middle nineteenth century and later; its office buildings are steel and glass monstrosities, generic enough to be at home in any office park anywhere; and its apartment complexes represent the only appearance of Maoist-style architecture in France. Where the Marais is grungy, grimy and beautiful, Neuilly is just grim, with wide dirty sidewalks, wide dirty streets, and cafes with the most dubious food in all of Paris.

I walked up Avenue Charles de Gaulle, a six-lane road teeming with automobiles. At the eastern end of this road is the Arc de Triomphe, a celebration of Napoleon's victory at Austerlitz; mirroring it, at the western end of the street, is La Grande Arche, an enormous hollow white cube celebrating the triumph of multinational commerce. La Grand Arche welcomes you into a skyscraper business community called La Défense, where the most giant of France's giant companies are headquartered. The whole avenue is a living memorial to one kind of conquest or another.

There are almost never pedestrians in the suburbs, just

endless stretches of concrete and asphalt, and I thumbed through my newspapers to avoid having to look directly at the soulless structures pressing down on me. I found no mention of Giselle anywhere in the news, which was good, but also no mention of Maximilien Luce.

The *International Herald-Tribune* occupies a slate-faced five-story building on rue des Graviers. I had spent a considerable amount of time in that building while working for the New York *Times*, and it was as good a reason as any to head off to a war.

I loped up the steps, through the main doors and past the three-foot-tall bronze owl that welcomes visitors to the lobby. The receptionist greeted me with a familiar, "Hey, Luke, how ya doin'," and I punched the button to call the elevator.

Jay Cutler had been the Chicago *Tribune*'s main man in Paris for many years before accepting an editorial job with the *Herald*. Since then, he sat more, smoked his pipe more and was gradually expanding around the middle. He always wore blue jeans and a suit vest, and he kept his gray-blonde hair slicked back with brilliantine. He knew the politics of Paris inside and out, and he had connections to most of the major players. He had a shrewd understanding of Parisian society, and if some mucky-muck had died recently and the estate had lost a priceless object, Jay might have heard something about it.

He stood up to greet me as I walked through the open door of his office. "Good to see you, Luke," he said, shaking my hand. "What the hell happened to you?"

"What do you mean?"

"Your eyes. I've seen less red in a Bloody Mary."

"Oh. A couple of physics professors did some math on my skull last night. That's what I came to talk to you about." Jay waved me into a seat. I closed his office door behind me, and we both sat down. "I need to speak to you in confidence."

"Fine. You in trouble?"

"I'm mixed up in something I don't really understand, though I'm in just a little bit at this point."

"Just a little bit is just enough. What's it about?"

"A painting." I told him what I knew about the provenance of the painting, without mentioning its location or the involvement of my friends, and I told him how the thugs had ransacked my place looking for it. "You know anything about someone missing a work of art?"

"Can't say that I do," Jay said. He leaned back, clasped his hands behind his head and stared at the wall behind me thoughtfully. "It certainly hasn't made the wires," he said, "and I haven't heard any talk of it around here, though art is not exactly my bailiwick. Just how did these guys get the impression that *you* might have such a painting?"

"I honestly don't know, and I don't know who they are. They came to my door and, unlike most people, they refused to credit my ignorance. Then they clubbed me and did a real number on my place."

"And you're sure it doesn't have anything to do with someone you pissed off in some war somewhere, maybe thinks you're connected to this painting that way?"

"I can't think of anyone. The crowd I usually meet in Indonesia isn't much interested in Post-Impressionism."

Jay shrugged. "If someone stole a painting from a museum, we'd certainly know about it. So, provided that such a painting actually *is* floating around loose somewhere, it must have belonged to a private collector."

"That's why I'm here. I need to know who these people are and how they found out who I am. You have any names you could give me in the art world, something that might connect the dots? Individuals, corporate collectors, maybe just a contact at one of the insurance companies that handle those kinds of things?"

"Not really. I don't think you'd want to start with families or insurance companies anyway. You'd never get anywhere. If I were you, I'd start with someone who knows about Maximilien Luce, and I've got just the guy for you. His name's Joseph Danton, over at the Musée D'Orsay. He's the curator of the Impressionist collection there—it's one of the largest collections of Impressionists in the world—and he pretty well knows who owns what and how they got it. He might not know about a theft if it just happened, but he would at least know who's supposed to have that painting, and that could point you in the right direction."

He found Joseph Danton's number in his rolodex and wrote it on a scrap of paper for me. I stood up to go.

"And you have no idea how you got mixed up in this?" Jay said, ironically, clearly dismissing this flimsy lie.

"If I did, I'd tell you, and then we'd both know," I said, maintaining the lie nevertheless.

"Uh-huh. Well, watch yourself, all right? And let me know what you find out. If nobody beats you bloody in the next few days, maybe I can buy you a drink and you can tell me what's really going on."

"Sure thing, Jay. Thanks."

* * * * *

As I walked back to the metro station, I dialed the museum and was miraculously connected directly to Joseph Danton. Jay had given me his private line! I made a mental note to send him a bottle of Glenfiddich.

When Danton answered, I mentioned Jay's name and briefly explained who I was and what I wanted, and the curator seemed enthusiastic about discussing Luce. He was not so enthusiastic, however, about seeing me that morning, and I decided, on behalf of Giselle, Benoît, Jean-Pierre and myself, to risk revealing my true purpose.

"I believe it's possible," I told Danton, "that I know where a stolen Maximilien Luce might be."

He told me to come right over, and I got back on the metro and headed east. Ten minutes later, I got out at the Jardin des Tuileries, just in time to join a group of Japanese tourists marching toward the Louvre. The tour guide's carefully rehearsed speech about the gardens appealed to me mainly because I didn't understand Japanese.

Past the Tuileries, I reached the Seine at Pont Royal, directly across the river from the Orsay, whose reflection shimmered in the placid green water. The Orsay Museum had originally been the main Paris station for the Orleans Railroad Line, which had gone out of business in the 1940s. When it had been converted to its present purpose in the 1970s, most of the original architecture had been preserved, and you would never know by its outer appearance that it was one of the most prominent museums of nineteenth century art in the world. It still looked exactly like the train station it had once been.

I crossed the bridge and thought about the river's path, as it made its way through downtown Paris, then flowed northwest to Herblay, Rouen and Honfleur before emptying into the Atlantic. Benoît's obsession with the river sometimes made sense to me—the Seine, like any river, was always the same and always changing, and this mystery of unvarying variability was seductive. When I was halfway across the bridge, a coal barge passed underneath me, and I stopped for a moment to watch it emerge on the far side, wondering if it was the very *péniche* that carried the painting, if Benoît was hiding below a tarp on the floor of the pilot's cabin.

A long line of people trailed down the sidewalk in front

of the Orsay, filing slowly toward the entrance. I took a moment to call Jean-Pierre and tell him what was happening. He had not heard from Benoît or Giselle, and I told him I would return to the Elephant after my conference with Danton, and we could then decide how to proceed.

I pushed and jostled my way past the tourists into the museum, where I found a security guard and explained my business. He guided me through a metal detector and then escorted me past the main galleries to a staircase that led to the staff suite on the third floor. I ascended and was shown to the Impressionist Curator's office.

Joseph Danton was six feet tall, with a salt-and-pepper afro so perfectly trimmed and symmetrical that it looked like a cast iron distilling pot. He had an open, friendly face, a firm handshake, and a perfectly tailored suit that, contrary to Parisian custom, had not been used as a picnic blanket recently. His lively brown eyes gave the impression that he was simultaneously attending to you and pondering a weighty and entirely unrelated matter.

His office was furnished in a sleek, modern style, with no art at all hanging on the walls. But then, I thought, if your waiting room contained hundreds of nineteenth century masterpieces, why would you need to decorate your office?

I thanked Danton for seeing me on such short notice. I then described the canvas I had seen for only a moment, and the one almost like it I had viewed on the internet, *La Seine à Herblay*.

"And you believe the painting you saw is of the same scene?" he asked, openly excited.

"I'm sure of it."

"Where did you see it? And what makes you believe it was stolen?"

"I saw it in a mountain village outside of Grozny, Chechnya," I lied. I explained that I was a war photographer and had just come back from doing a story on the separatist guerrilla movement there. "There's a tremendous black market in Chechnya, mostly drugs and weapons but also looted merchandise, jewelry and gold and so on. I had a local guide who knew some of the bazaars, and one of them held this canvas—it was so unusual, in that context, that I remembered it and looked it up when I came back." This lie was not as far-fetched as it might at first seem. Once, at an underground market in Uruguay, I had found a Stradivarius.

"And you're sure it was a genuine Luce? Not an imitation or a forgery?"

"That I'm not sure of, though it wasn't a likely place for forgeries. Honestly, I had never heard of Luce before, and I doubt anybody at that bazaar had either, so whether it was genuine or not wouldn't have made much difference to the price. I've seen this lots of times in wars—somebody sacks a place and just steals everything that might be valuable, whether they know its actual value or not."

"Well, the painting that you describe certainly could be valuable, for a variety of reasons—provided that it's genuine."

"I just know that the style looked the same as the one I saw on the internet, and the signature looked the same."

"We actually have that painting here in our collection, the one you saw on the internet. Perhaps you'd like to see it in person, as a comparison."

"You have *La Seine à Herblay* here?"

"I should say we have one of them. There were three that Luce painted in a series near Herblay."

"Then you think the one I saw might actually be one of his? Would it be worth returning to Grozny for?" If Danton thought the painting was worth retrieving from war-torn Chechnya, then it would certainly be worth tracking down on a barge just outside the museum.

"It's an irreplaceable work of art, Mr. Johnson." Danton spread his hands to indicate that no risk, no price was too great for the acquisition of such a rare painting. He then gave me a brief history of Maximilien Luce.

Luce was the son of an undistinguished City of Paris employee. In his youth, he had trained as a wood engraver, but he soon fell in with a group of Impressionist painters, especially Pisarro, Manet and Bazille, and he began painting and drawing. His early paintings were typical of the Impressionist style, but then Luce, Signac and Seurat began using small dots of paint instead of brush strokes; the dots imitated the structure of the eye's rods and cones and created primary colors by blending secondary colors. This was the birth of a style called Pointillism, and that was the style that *La Seine à Herblay* had been painted in. Furthermore, Danton said, Luce was a far left wing Socialist and one of the fathers of Social Realist painting: unlike most of his contemporaries, he depicted scenes of laborers at work and showed profound sympathy for the plight of the poor and outcast.

"But, specifically," I said, "what else can you tell me about his paintings of the Seine?"

"The Seine appears in many of Luce's paintings," Danton said, "but often as a backdrop to some human activity along its banks, especially factory labor or dock work. He did have a small cottage at Rolleboise, just outside of Paris, and his paintings of the river there are more pastoral and less political. The scenes he did at Herblay are among that same variety, more idyllic: florid fields and calm waters, no people or animals, and a highly mannered style, with vivid dots of paint.

"The reason your painting might be especially interesting," Danton continued, "is that it was thought to have been lost in the Second World War. As I said, Luce did three paintings of the Seine at Herblay, but the Orsay has the only one known to still exist. One of the series was destroyed in an air raid on Mantes-la-Jolie late in the war, by allied forces. The other has been missing since the German occupation of France and has never been recovered.

"Many art works stolen during the war have been found and returned to their rightful owners, or their destruction has been documented in some way. But a few are still unaccounted for. If the painting you saw is genuine, it would be a major discovery—a major *recovery*. Do you think there's any way you could find it again?"

"How much might it be worth if I did?"

"To the art world, it would be invaluable," Danton said, with obvious disdain for the greed behind my question. "In monetary terms. . . well. . . the most a Luce has ever brought at auction is a little under a million euros. Given the unusual circumstances around the discovery of this painting, it might generate marginally increased value, but still, the question of authenticate ownership would have to be addressed—it was stolen from the Musée de L'Hôtel-Dieu by the Nazis and would be considered a national treasure of France."

This, at least, confirmed what I had always known about Giselle—she knew the value of things and had exceptional taste. I couldn't wait to see her again and learn how she had come across a long-lost national treasure, and especially how she had managed to steal it. And, for that matter, why? Most antique dealers would be happy with the fat commission selling such a painting might bring.

"Could I see the painting now," I asked, "the version of *La Seine à Herblay* in your gallery?"

"Certainly."

Danton escorted me out of his office and toward the Impressionist wing of the Orsay. As we walked back into the public areas, he carried on a disquisition about his theories of art ownership, the responsibility of individuals to respect their culture, and the value to the public of having access to works representing significant cultural developments. Danton, of course, would insist that any such recovered painting be handed over to a museum, but I had read accounts of Napoleon's campaigns and remembered how many great works of art he had stolen in wars of conquest. Obviously, Napoleon had never returned them and now they resided across the river in the Louvre, and they, too, were national treasures of France. I wondered how morally correct the acquisition of the paintings and sculptures in the Orsay had been, as we passed one masterpiece after another, and what moral principle I might be obliged to follow regarding the Luce.

The galleries were crowded with tourists, and Danton led me slowly up several staircases at one end of the museum. We reached level five, where the Picassos, Signacs and Renoirs were housed. Everyone felt the authority of Danton's presence, and a path cleared in front of him wherever he walked.

As we stepped into the small, brightly lit room holding *La Seine à Herblay*, my cell phone rang. I immediately grabbed it out of my pocket, but Danton frowned at me and said definitively, "No cell phones in the galleries, Mr. Johnson." I looked at the phone's digital read-out—the incoming call was from Giselle!

I let it ring again—it was absolutely imperative that I speak with her, but I didn't wish to anger Danton. The second ring displeased him enough. "Mr. Johnson!" he said sternly. Everyone was now looking at us, and Danton was looking at everyone else, embarrassed—in the staid environment of the museum, this was close to a riot, and a museum guard was making his way toward me.

I cursed silently and shut the phone off, hoping Giselle

would leave her whereabouts on my voice mail. I slipped the phone back into my pocket. Danton said, "Thank you," and the crowd returned to its glassy-eyed gazing.

"This painting is important to our collection," Danton said, "because it looks back to the stylistic concerns of the Impressionists but forward to innovations in Pointillism and Expressionism. Luce is not a major figure in the genesis of these later styles, but he plays a role in developing both of them, and his thematic concerns would eventually become cornerstones for certain kinds of Realism. So while he doesn't possess the genius of a Seurat, he is a pivotal figure." Danton leaned toward me for emphasis, and for the first time I noticed a kind of avarice in his tone. "Another example of Luce's work from this period would be a significant addition to any gallery's collection."

I studied *La Seine à Herblay*, and, discounting for the moment the possibility of a clever forgery, I believed that the painting I had held yesterday evening was indeed the work of Maximilien Luce. The perspectives were slightly different in each: the one I had seen at the Elephant featured the river at a snaking-S bend, where in this one the river made a more sweeping curve; the patterns of the wildflowers were different but featured the same basic color schemes; and this one was painted from higher up on a hill than the one Giselle had stolen. However, they used the same style, the same sensibility of light, and there was no mistaking the similarity of the terrain. The painting Benoît was sitting on (probably literally) was almost certainly of Herblay.

A large group of English schoolchildren trooped around us while Danton looked at me curiously, without moving a muscle. A guide began explaining the Luce painting in condescendingly stentorian English.

"Well, Mr. Johnson?"

"I think it's the same."

"And would you be willing to give me details of the painting's location? As much as you remember them? I could pass the information along to Interpol, and we may at least have some chance of recovering it." I hesitated, and Danton motioned for me to follow him out of the gallery. "You would be doing a great public service," he said softly, "and I'm sure the French government would show its appreciation in some *measurable* way."

We pushed through the tourists, who were intent on avoiding the actual French countryside by viewing representations of it inside an old train station. Danton led me back down the staircases, in the direction of his office, but I had learned what I needed to learn from him, and I wanted to get out of the museum and call Giselle.

"Mr. Danton," I said, as we reached the main concourse, "I'd like to thank you for your help. But I'm afraid that revealing my contacts in Chechnya could place them in great danger." I shook his hand.

"If you really want to thank me, you'll help recover that painting." As I prepared to depart, a quiet desperation grew in his eyes, and it seemed that Danton was much more excited about the prospect of the missing Luce than I was. I realized that if he could play a role in finding it and perhaps even bringing it to the Orsay, he would become a hero in the art world—it might even vault an already distinguished career into renown. He gave me his card. "I urge you to do the right thing with what you know, Mr. Johnson."

I thanked him again and left him standing in the tour groups' meeting area. On my way out the main exit, I passed a tacky gift shop, which displayed 1000-piece puzzles of Manet paintings and garish neckties with Picasso reproductions silk-screened onto them. I wondered if that was Danton's idea of being responsible to European culture.

5

Giselle

Outside on Quai Anatole France, the four-lane street that runs along the Left Bank in front of the museum, I activated my phone and retrieved Giselle's message. She said she had just spoken with Jean-Pierre and knew that I was at the Orsay, and if I could manage it at all I should meet her in front of the museum in half an hour. It was now twenty minutes since she had left the message, so I peered down the quay, looking for her BMW.

Though traffic along this street usually moves briskly, it gets congested with pedestrian crossings right in front of the Orsay. I jogged a little upriver, hoping Giselle might spot me easier away from the crowds of tourists.

After ten minutes, Giselle had not appeared, and after twenty minutes, I began to think something unfortunate had happened. I was just dialing Jean-Pierre when a horn blared insistently. I looked up but could not find Giselle's little red sports car in the traffic. The honk came again, and I spotted Giselle waving frantically from an ancient rusted-out cream-colored Citroën—the last car I ever expected to see her in. She was in the middle of the street, and now she swerved almost into the car next to her, trying to change into the curbside lane to pick me up. Her junker sedan bulled through the snarl, and the drivers of nicer cars, fearing for their fenders and paint, cleared a path. She stopped cold right in front of me, and the drivers behind her honked and yelled. *"Putain! Va te faire foutre!"* I jumped into the back seat, she hit the accelerator, and we lurched back into the flow of traffic.

"Am I ever glad to see you!" she said.

"Likewise." I shimmied into the front passenger seat.

She was wearing the same clothes from the night before, when she had run frantically into the Happy Elephant, except that her conservative, ankle-length skirt was now a mini-skirt, thanks to a ragged alteration, and her blouse was smeared with dirt and much the worse for wear. The usually spindly laugh lines around her eyes now appeared deep and unhappy.

"Where'd you get this barrel of bolts?" I asked.

"I had to trade down. One of the many bad trades I've made in the last twenty-four hours."

She flipped on her blinker to change lanes but once again did not wait for traffic to clear and cut off a motorscooter in the process. She repeated this maneuver twice more to get into the far right lane, leaving a wake of fist-waving motorists choking in the Citroën's thick blue exhaust. She made a helter-skelter turn onto the Concorde Bridge.

"Since you've talked to Jean-Pierre, I suppose you know that Benoît has the painting?"

"I do." She barely made the green light at the other end of the bridge, and then turned right on the Quai des Tuileries. We were now on the opposite side of the Seine from the Orsay, heading in the opposite direction. She checked her rearview mirror.

"And you know that no one knows where Benoît is?"

Giselle sighed. " I know." She checked her rearview mirror again. "Do you see a black Mercedes sedan following us?"

I turned in my seat. "No."

"Keep looking."

I kept looking as we passed the Louvre and La Samaritaine department store. "I don't see a black Mercedes."

"Good. I think I lost them back on Saint-Germain."

"You're kidding?" I wondered how she could ever have out-raced a high-performance sedan in this oil-spewing wreck.

"I'm heading for your apartment—is that all right?"

"For what?"

"Just to lay low for a while. I need to rest, get my head together."

"Well, no, we can't go to my apartment, then, not if you're looking for a safe haven. Didn't Jean-Pierre tell you?"

Giselle looked exasperated. "I only spoke to him for a moment before I had to take some evasive action. What should he have told me?"

I recounted the story of the break-in and then filled in the other gaps that her brief conversation with Jean-Pierre had left. Once I had brought her up to date on the story as I knew it, I asked her to do the same for me. "Such as, just for starters, who *were* those guys who beat me up?"

"I'm honestly not sure. I've kind of lost track of every-body." She ran her fingers through her hair and I thought she might cry.

"All right," I said. "Let's think of someplace safe to go."

* * * * *

One of the many differences between Séverine's apartment and mine is that Séverine can't see everything she owns just by turning her head. Her family has owned a four-room flat on Île Saint Louis for generations, and as a successful designer she can afford to furnish it in style. Île Saint Louis is one of two islands (along with Île de la Cité) that sit in the middle of the Seine and form the heart of downtown Paris; it also con-tains some of the most expensive real estate in Europe. From Séverine's balcony, three stories above the river, the apartment looks across a channel of the Seine to the back of Notre Dame

Cathedral on the other island. Montaigne once had an apartment in Séverine's building, and the families who live there now continue to be among Paris's commercial and intellectual elite.

Giselle found a parking spot on rue le Regrattier, half a block from Séverine's door. In the accepted Parisian fashion, I stood watch while she rammed the bumpers of the cars in front and behind her, parallel parking. She checked up and down the street for the black Mercedes, but neither of us saw any suspicious cars, and we walked quickly to Séverine's building. I punched in the security codes to open the outside doors, and then we climbed to the third floor.

Hanging on the wall of the staircase just before you reach Séverine's landing is an old but nondescript metal crucifix: if you remove it from the wall and press down on the nail in Christ's left hand, a small panel opens in the back of his body, revealing a hidden compartment. A spare key to Séverine's place is concealed there, and I used it to open her door and let us in.

"You know, I sold her that crucifix," Giselle said, as she collapsed onto the day-bed in Séverine's living room. "I found it at the Galadette flea market—supposedly, it belonged to Cardinal Richelieu."

"You want a coffee or a vodka tonic?" I went into the kitchen.

"Vodka, hold the tonic. You think Séverine has anything I could wear?"

"I'm sure we can find you a wrap or a sari or something that will fit. You'll have to prepare yourself to be noticed, though—Séverine doesn't have clothes you can exactly hide in." I returned to the living room with a mineral water for myself and a highball of vodka for Giselle. "First, of course, you have to tell me what the hell is going on."

Giselle gulped at the vodka and flopped back onto the day-bed. I sat down next to her and waited.

"What would you like to know first?" she asked. "About the painting? Or where I got it? Or who's chasing me?"

"Don't be coy. You've put all of us in a terrible position. You got me beaten up. Benoît is on the lamb. Jean-Pierre. . . well, you know how Jean-Pierre feels, and now he's a criminal accessory! We're *all* out on a limb for you."

She looked at me, simultaneously self-pitying and apologetic, and downed the rest of her drink in one go. She coughed down the alcohol and set the empty glass on the table at her elbow, and then she studied her feet for a long time.

"I'm sorry," she said. When she looked up again, her lower lip was trembling. "I made a bad mistake." A heavy tear formed in the corner of her left eye, swelled, and then rolled slowly down her cheek. A second tear followed it, almost in slow-motion, while she continued to stare into my eyes. I could feel her collapsing silently inside, exhausted and guilty. She was suddenly wracked by a tremendous sob.

I took her in my arms and rubbed her back and told her everything was all right, though that lie was more for me than for her. I held her and rocked her for a few minutes, until the relief that she felt at finally being safe had liberated all of her panic, and she stopped crying. I got her some tissues from the bathroom. As she dried her eyes, the air in the room became heavy again—her relief disappeared as quickly as it had come, and the gravity of her situation weighed down on her. She was an emotional wreck, volatile and insecure and utterly exhausted.

I poured her another vodka and then sat down beside her, noticing, for the first time since I had met her, how beautiful she was. No, that's not quite true: Giselle is a physically attractive woman, and she's also clear-minded and strong-willed—I knew already that she was beautiful. But I had never personally been attracted to her before. She had always needed to be in control, self-sufficient and independent, and in the six years I had known her, I had never once seen a chink in her armor. In the last day, however, she had not only lost control but come completely unhinged, and seeing her this way, strung out, pathetic and helpless, made me want to protect her and love her. She looked positively awful and I wanted to hold her and kiss her.

She sipped her vodka. I touched her shoulder and moved toward her, but when she looked into my eyes, the fear and uncertainty in them overwhelmed me. She seemed on the verge of tears again.

"Why don't you tell me how you got the painting?" I said.

She held my gaze a moment longer, and I felt her sensing my attraction. Another moment and we might have kissed, but she sighed and looked down at her lap. Like a reluctant schoolgirl forced to perform in a class play, she began reciting her story flatly, her tone dejected and world-weary.

* * * * *

Giselle's parents had been antique dealers and her grandparents had been antique dealers, and before that her family had been cabinet makers—this is still the rule with French families, that small businesses and apartments and reputations pass from one generation to the next, as they used to everywhere. So when Giselle inherited her antique shop from her mother, she also inherited its prestige and wealthy clientele. She would often be invited to appraise old-money estates with priceless heirlooms, choice crystal, rare documents and exquisitely maintained fifteenth-century furniture—items that other antique dealers, whose connections were less stellar, would give their eyeteeth for. Once you have a reputation in Paris society circles, doors open for you, and Giselle was used to walking through them.

However, her sensibility was not her mother's. Giselle learned the antique trade inside and out and was well-versed in a wide variety of jewelry, art and furniture specialties, but she leaned more in her personal tastes toward beer and action movies than vintage cognac and ballet. I got to know her only because she liked hole-in-the-wall bars like the Happy Elephant rather than swanky *palais* like the Crillon, and in that way, she lived a double life: absolutely proper, with unimpeachable taste and etiquette around her clients; more liberated and carefree in her social life, at home in the company of a garbage collector like Benoît. Compared to my war correspondent friends, she was still an uptight functionary of high society, but next to the old aristocracy, she was practically an anarchist.

To me, Giselle had always seemed too controlling and prim, the opposite that balanced Benoît's passionate dissolution in our little group at the Elephant. She was a fun drinking partner who told interesting stories about a life I had no access to, dishing gossip about the super-rich and reveling in my irreverence toward her clients, but I had thought that that was where the complexity of her character ended.

After her mother died, Giselle had gradually let her business decline. She was not nearly as aggressive in pursuing new clients, not nearly as willing to hobnob with the right people at social events, and though she knew the value of things she would sometimes make dubious financial choices expressly to defy that value.

"Some days," she said, "I really hated the fact that someone would pay ten thousand euros for a Lalique figurine. It seemed repulsive somehow that something so beautiful could be valued against other kinds of things—like, with ten thousand euros you could buy a compact car or a Safari vacation in Kenya or this delicate little crystal figurine." She paused for a drink of vodka. "It's hard to explain in a way that makes sense, even to myself, but the way my clients feel about beautiful things is just offensive to me—morally, aesthetically, in every way. They feel as if they *deserve* beauty in their lives, but they're so saturated with it that they never really see it. They want their living rooms furnished entirely in Empire, and because their knick-knacks can't clash with their divans, they spend hundreds of thousands of dollars for magnificent things to put on their incidental shelves. Which they never even look at. There are poor people who would *worship* a Lalique figurine, who would give everything they had just to touch one."

These sentiments surprised me, especially in the way they echoed Joseph Danton's insistence that art be available to the public, where it could be appreciated for its true worth (whatever that was supposed to be). Giselle had always presented herself as concerned first and foremost with the monetary value of things, with their rarity and status, and her own home was crowded with insanely expensive furniture, ancient tapestries and recherché bibelots. But, she said, after she took over her mother's shop, she would often sell items at a loss—people would come into the shop and fall in love with a breakfront or a dressing table that they couldn't possibly afford, and she would sell it to them for much less than she had paid because she respected their love for the items.

Over the years, she had assuaged her conflicted feelings about monetary values by losing great sums of money in giveaways and discounts. She confessed that this made no sense to her logically—she had become a kind of Robin Hood antique dealer, redistributing value from the super-rich to the middle-class at her own expense—but it had become not just a weakness but a psychological compulsion, and now her shop was going under as a result. She had long been selling off the personal treasures her mother had left her in order to maintain appearances, but she was running out of private heirlooms. She had let her business slip to the point where it no longer even supported her, and she was facing the possibility of liquidation.

So she'd been relieved to get a call the week before last from the Dumesnil family, landed gentry with certifiably blue blood going back to the thirteen hundreds. Countess Dumesnil had died at the age of ninety-three, and the family was consolidating her holdings and selling some of her possessions. They had done business with Giselle's mother, and they called Giselle to appraise the estate, which included an apartment in Paris near the Luxembourg Gardens and the family castle outside of Reims.

An appraisal of such an estate, just by itself, is not cheap, and the infusion of cash this brought Giselle was welcome. However, when she realized the extraordinary nature of the artifacts in the castle, she conceived a plan that would net her much more than an appraisal fee and some sales commissions—a plan that could not only make her solvent again but might keep her head above water for the rest of her life.

On the first day of her appraisal, at the castle outside of Reims, the dead Countess's son—the new Count Dumesnil—was introducing Giselle to the many items to be sold. As they toured the castle, the Count got an urgent call and left Giselle alone, to begin a catalog of items by herself. He was away long enough that Giselle started moving from room to room, exploring the full extent of the task at hand, and that's when her life began to turn on its head.

She wandered quite haphazardly into a room at the very heart of the Dumesnil castle, and she discovered not only the

Maximilien Luce painting on the wall, but a sculpture by Rodin, some Art Nouveau glassware, a Fabergé egg and some ancient clothing behind glass. Not realizing the importance of these items at the time, she began making notes about them for appraisal. When Count Dumesnil finished his business and realized where she was, he came rushing in and anxiously herded her out into the hall. He told her those items would not be part of the sale, and he snatched the notes Giselle had made and ripped them up.

"This isn't the most unusual thing in the world," Giselle said. "Everyone has eccentricities, especially about their private stuff in their own homes, and the rich are of course more eccentric than anyone. I didn't really think much of it at the time, beyond trying not to be offended by the simple crassness of his actions. Besides, the room was open—I just walked right in—and I hardly imagined that the Count, knowing I was coming, would leave any dark family secrets lying out in plain view. So I just wrote it off as a peculiarity.

"We went back into the rooms he wanted appraised, and over the next few days, I spent a lot of time at the castle. There were no more incidents like that and we didn't discuss it, but afterward he always hovered over me, no matter how tedious my task. He never left me alone. Between the paranoid hovering and the anxiety I remembered on the Count's face when he'd discovered me in that one particular room, my feeling that something was wrong got stronger and stronger. So I started investigating the artifacts from that room."

Giselle has an excellent memory, and she reconstructed a list of items housed in the forbidden chamber. When she began searching catalogs and making phone calls, she discovered that every single thing in that room was officially missing, stolen or presumed destroyed in the Second World War. She couldn't understand how the Dumesnil family could have come into possession of such cultural treasures, with such similar histories of theft, if they hadn't stolen them themselves, and some research into the family's background produced circumstantial confirmation of her suspicion.

During the war, Giselle discovered, the Dumesnil family had collaborated with the Nazis through the Vichy government. Though this embarrassing fact had quickly been hushed up, thanks to the family's centuries-old position of power, the Dumesnils fell out of political influence and their standing in society became ambiguous. Time and lavish charitable contributions had helped restore some of the prestige of the family name, and the success of the current Count in his career as a biomedical researcher had eventually allowed Paris society to paper over the family's treasonous behavior. But no one knew that the old Countess Dumesnil had held onto the plundered artwork she had somehow acquired during the war, and such a revelation now would surely ruin the family.

"That's when I decided I could take advantage of the situation," Giselle said. "If they lost a painting or a statue or that Fabergé egg, they could hardly go to the police. They couldn't tell anyone at all, and I could sell whatever I took and get back on my feet."

She researched each item as carefully as her memory, the historical records and the valuation guides would allow, and she decided that the Luce painting had the biggest bang for the buck, would be the easiest to sell on the black market and would not be the worst possible loss to the Dumesnil collection. Knowing that the Count would be furious, she decided to take only the one thing and afterward try to reach a truce with the family, based on their mutual knowledge of each other's crimes.

"I see now how foolish that was," she said. "But at the time I was thinking, 'here's all of this stolen art, and I'm sinking myself financially because I'm giving art away'—it seemed like a cosmic revenge on the Count and a validation of what I'd been doing at the same time." She sighed. "I thought the universe was saying, what comes around, goes around. You give away art, and now the forces of karma are going to give some art back to you. It makes no sense, I know. . ." She drained down her second vodka. "Anyway, the Count seemed so weird and frail—how dangerous could this old guy be, I thought. A Nazi collaborator, right?" she said ironically. "How dangerous could someone like *that* be? I guess I was just coming to the end of my rope and didn't have any other ideas."

She asked if there were any more liquor. I returned to the kitchen and brought back the bottle.

"I put out feelers to some people I knew, people who might have connections to the black market," she continued. "I've never dealt in stolen stuff before, but when you work with items this rare and valuable, you hear things sometimes, and people are always hedging, trading under the table, whispering about the one painting they'd do anything for if they could only get their hands on it, the one lithograph or signed document or caliph's scimitar or whatever that would be beyond price. People want different things, but they want and they want, and they'll pay for what they want."

Giselle located a man who knew a "private" art collector interested in the Luce, and she arranged the sale. The only hurdle left was actually stealing it, which she had done just three hours before she had given it to me at the Happy Elephant.

"What I needed," she said, "was a chance to be alone in the castle. I was almost finished with the appraisal, so I would soon have less and less reason to go out there. The Count had decided to let me arrange the sale of some of the items, so I decided to finish the appraisal, make some sales in a show of good faith, and then show up unexpectedly one day at the castle when I knew the Count wouldn't be there. In that way, I hoped to return to that room, get the painting out somehow and get the hell out of there, and hopefully give myself an hour or two before the Count found out about it. That would be enough time to get the painting to my contact and get the money into my bank, and then I could negotiate a little mutual blackmail with the Count."

This plan, of course, sounded completely hopeless—it wasn't really a plan at all. But one thing I've learned from all the war zones I've survived is that desire, and the willingness to act on it, count for almost as much as the feasibility of your schemes. The primary trouble with a bad scheme, however, is not that it might fail, but that it might succeed against all odds and then leave you in an untenable position. That's often the story of an armed skirmish—a force will capture a target through the sheer audacity of its assault, but that same audacity cannot hold the ground they have taken.

Giselle's simple plan, as much as it actually was a plan, worked, but only sort of. She did arrive at the castle one day while the Count was in Dijon, and she even managed to slip alone down a series of dark halls and into the heart of the castle, where the stolen art was kept. This time, however, the door was locked, but she was even prepared for that: as an antique-dealing family, Giselle and her parents and grandparents had a store of old keys, wax impressions of locks and delicate tools useful for manipulating tumblers and rods, and Giselle had noted the kinds of locks the Count used throughout his castle. She had come prepared with a lockpick set, the sheer variety of whose instruments would have impressed James Bond; however, Agent 007 would certainly not have approved of the size and weight of Giselle's kit, nor would he have carried the huge alligator-skin purse necessary to conceal it. The kit also had a more essential drawback: it didn't work. The locks on the door to the secret chamber were specially designed, state-of-the-art, and none of Giselle's keys or picks matched it.

At that point, the sensible move would have been to give up, go home and sell the antique shop. But another thing I've found in battle situations is that the same crazy willpower necessary to conceive and then initiate a bad plan will also make it difficult to give the objective up, once the wheels are in motion. In the heat of the moment, the possibility of quitting, of just admitting defeat and running away, sometimes disappears from your mind, and you instead generate ever more desperate and unlikely ideas for making the plan work. This is what happened to Giselle.

With her black market contact waiting for her and, in her mind, the whole future of her antique shop hanging in the balance, she committed a truly desperate act, one not just of larceny but of violence. She returned to the castle's main salons, found the butler, and contrived through an utterly transparent but successful ruse to get him to turn his back to her. Then she conked him over the head with a brass candlestick.

"It was thrilling and sickening at the same time," Giselle confessed, slurring her words slightly as she made her way through her third vodka. "He just crumpled to the floor, and it was at that point that I realized everything had changed. My whole life had changed, and the whole plan seemed exactly as stupid as it always was. But there was something about it—standing over this old guy with a weapon in my hand, having him totally at my mercy—that made me continue. I could see clearly at that moment that there was no way I could ever get away with it, and now the crimes were adding up, but it was such a rush, the power of it, the freedom. It was like all my other problems now amounted to nothing, and the only thing that mattered was getting that painting."

The butler was not alone in the castle: the Count had a

small kitchen staff, a groundskeeper, and a cleaning woman, so leaving an unconscious servant lying out on the floor was likely to attract attention. Even if nobody saw Giselle herself running down a hall awkwardly, with a painting pinned to the inside of her skirt ("Can you think of a *less* practical way of hiding a painting?" she asked), they would soon discover the poleaxed butler and sound the alarm. Nevertheless, Giselle lifted the butler's keys and ran as fast as her ankle-length skirt would allow back to the stolen artifacts room.

Amazingly, one of the keys actually opened the door. I say "amazingly" because, if I were a Nazi collaborator with millions of dollars of looted art in my rec room, I wouldn't give my butler a key. But people are funny.

Giselle opened the door, cut the painting out of its frame, pinned it beneath her clothes and then locked the door behind her again. The butler was still on the floor when she returned, so she put his keys back in his pocket, then fled to her BMW and raced away.

"At that point," she said, "I had really done it, and I got tunnel vision. All I could think of was meeting my contact, getting the money, and getting away with it. And then, after all the zeros had lined up in my bank account, I would see how the chips had fallen. On the drive from Reims to Paris, I began to think it would actually turn out all right."

When she arrived at the rendezvous spot, however, not only was her black market contact not there, but two other men were waiting for her. She had never seen them before, but they knew her—they got the jump on her, and she barely managed to escape. She assumed, she said, that these were the same men who had beaten me up, but she couldn't be sure.

"And the rest," she said, with a theatrical wave of her hand, "is history." She took another big swallow of vodka.

"Not quite," I said. "Were the two men who met you—the

men who beat me up—were they sent by the Count? Could he have gotten word of your little escapade and sent someone to ambush you so quickly?"

"I don't know. For that matter, I don't know what happened to my black market guy, either. Or even if he's still alive."

"And what happened to your Z8? How did you wind up with that Citroën?"

"Oh, God," she said, exhausted. "That's another long story." She leaned into me and rested her head on my shoulder. "Can I just relax for a minute?"

"All right." I relieved her of her vodka and kissed the top of her head, and then helped her to her feet and guided her toward the bathroom. "I'll draw you a bath. While you get cleaned up, I'll call Jean-Pierre and see if we can track down Benoît. Maybe we can think of a way to get you out of this." She thanked me and hugged me, a little bit longer than simple gratitude would require.

"But you won't leave this apartment until you tell me the rest of the story."

* * * * *

I reached Jean-Pierre at the Happy Elephant, where he reported that he'd been standing guard with a tire iron, his cell phone programmed to dial the police. The Elephant was beginning to remind me of a command post or bureau station, the central information headquarters of the whole operation—whatever the hell the operation was.

"I just had a visitor," Jean-Pierre said, "a messenger from one of the barges. He brought word from Benoît."

"Why didn't Benoît come himself? Where is he?"

"He's still on a barge, I suppose."

"Is he in trouble?"

"Not that I know of. Maybe he's just frightened and hiding out somewhere, or maybe he has a master plan. You never know with Benoît."

"And he can't just phone you, of course! Nothing can be simple."

"I guess this is how bargemen communicate," said Jean-Pierre. "Word of mouth."

"You can't get a cell phone on a barge?"

"Look, do you want to hear the message or not?"

Jean-Pierre never snaps at people, and I realized then that his nerves must have been frayed. My complaints about Benoît were apparently not helping him relax.

"About half an hour ago," he said, "a guy in a black watchman's cap showed up here. The message was that we could find what we were looking for '*en Le Fascinage*.'"

"*Le Fascinage*?" I said. "What is that—the name of a barge?"

"I don't know."

"And what are we looking for—Benoît or the painting? Or both?"

"That was the whole message—'you can find what you're looking for *en Le fascinage*.' I questioned the guy, but he said that was all he had to tell me. He wouldn't say if he got the message directly from Benoît or some other bargee, he wouldn't say who he was or how he knew Benoît—he just clammed up. He looked like a much tougher customer than those two who came to the bar last night."

"Those boatmen have their own enforcers," I agreed.

"Anyway," Jean-Pierre continued, "he just stood here and stared at me for a while, stone-faced. I'm not sure what the etiquette is when you receive a cryptic message, so I finally gave him a beer. He downed it and left, and that's all I know."

I told Jean-Pierre that I had found Giselle and that we were both safe for the moment, but I wasn't going to tell him where we were. That would save him from obstructing a police investigation, if the *gendarmes* should question him about Giselle's whereabouts. "What address did Benoît head off to last night, with the police?" I asked. Jean-Pierre said it was somewhere along a quay called Fernand Saguet. "All right, I'll call you if there's any news to report," I said, "and definitely call me if you hear anything else."

I hung up, opened the door to Séverine's balcony and stepped outside. The gardenias in Séverine's flowerbeds were in full bloom. I leaned against the railing, and looked out at the sky and the dark green river. Across the channel on the Île de la Cité, in the little gardens behind Notre Dame, tourists were strolling and laughing and snapping photos of the cathedral. Below Séverine's balcony, on this side of the channel, people were heading up the Quai d'Orleans toward the restaurants and brasseries on rue des Deux Ponts; a juggler with a black valise opened in front of him was busking for change on the cobblestone sidewalk. Dark patches of clouds were beginning to encroach here and there on an otherwise sunny day, and the air felt uncertain and muggy, as if a storm were building. I stared into the Seine—somewhere on that river, Benoît and *Le Fascinage* were waiting with the Luce, and now it was just a matter of finding them.

Of course, it was unclear what we were supposed to do once we had the painting again. Jean-Pierre would say turn it over to the police. Joseph Danton would say give it to the Orsay Museum. Giselle might still want to sell it on the black market. The Count would certainly want the thing back. As for me, I remained uncommitted to any particular outcome. The only people who could rightly claim ownership of the painting were Maximilien Luce, whoever he sold it to in the first place, or the Musée de L'Hôtel-Dieu, which the Nazis had stolen it from. Since none of those people were presently involved, the matter seemed muddy.

At an intellectual level, the moral questions about who owned art and the proper function of beauty in society were interesting; but I had to admit that a share of the million euros we might get on the black market also had its attraction. This was sixty-year-old war booty, after all, and I had seen enough property change hands "illegally" that I was no longer sure where the lines could be drawn. If I helped sell a painting stolen by Vichy collaborators, was I implicated in the crimes of the Nazis? Or just Giselle's crimes? Was the butler's cracked head my responsibility? And what about *my* cracked head—who was going to pay for that?

I turned away from the balcony and stepped back inside. I could hear Giselle splashing in the bathtub, and the thought of her slim body naked in the warm soapy water, her short blonde hair wet and dark against her head, her haggard eyes looking up at me gratefully, made my heart clinch. Something about the secret life she had been leading, so controlled and rectilinear on the outside, so conflicted and self-destructive on the inside, gave her a tragic depth in my mind. She *was* like a Robin Hood, sort of, but the ironies and complexities of her situation, of her crime, made her an erotic shadow of that legend, and I'd have bet any amount that she looked better in tights than the Merry Men. I decided to switch from mineral water to vodka.

Soon, I heard water draining out of the tub, and I realized that Giselle must have left the bathroom door open. I walked toward it—the door was indeed open a crack, and I felt steam wafting out. Giselle passed in front of the door, her shoulders and long legs bare and wet, a red towel wrapped around her body. She bent down to examine the skin products in Séverine's little cabinet, and she caught me looking at her.

Our eyes met, and she stood up slowly, adjusting the towel where it was tucked in over her left breast. "Do you know where *your girlfriend* keeps her body oils?"

The question was a provocation, not a warning. Giselle has known Séverine as long as she's known me, and she's spent more time with Séverine: whenever I'm out of the country, Séverine and Giselle often spend evenings together at the Elephant, and I had never heard Giselle refer to Séverine as "my girlfriend" before.

"What you want," I said, "is right in front of you."

She licked her lips. "Perhaps you could show me." Deliberately, studiously, she opened the saturated red towel with both hands, until her entire body was exposed. Then she lowered her arms to her sides and let the towel fall to the floor.

Despite the tendency of French fashions to follow the contours of the body, I had never realized before just how full Giselle's breasts were and would never have predicted that they could be so pendulous and inviting. She had bruises on her arms and thighs, and there was an angry red mark, like a rope burn, on her stomach; all of which, in some way I could not understand, made her more attractive. I set my vodka on an incidental table in the hall and walked into the bathroom.

She put her hand on my chest. I cupped her right breast and gently caressed her shoulder and arm, lingering on the yellowing bruise on her right bicep. She drew in a sharp breath of pain and then put her arms around my neck and kissed me. I was surprised at how soft and yielding her lips were, so different from the hard, calculating idea of Giselle I had in my mind. I pulled her body into mine and pressed her against me, as my hands massaged the length of her back and wrapped around her ass. She started to lift her leg over mine, but I pulled away and stepped back.

I knelt down in front of her and smelled her flesh, still

warm and supple from the hot water, perfumed by Séverine's lavender bubble bath. I kissed her belly, then selected a jasmine body oil from the bottom shelf of the vanity and held it up to her.

"I believe this is what you were looking for."

I unscrewed the cap, poured a generous amount into my hand and began rubbing it into the back of Giselle's thighs and ass as I kissed and licked her belly and nuzzled my nose into the triangle of hair between her legs. Everything about Giselle's body was unexpected, including the musky, spicy smell and taste of her, so unlike the perfectly unsullied blandness I would have anticipated.

She ran her fingers through my hair as I kneaded body oil into her flesh, as my fingers found the moist opening between her legs, and then she pulled me by the ears to my feet and put her tongue in my mouth. She pushed me back, out of the bathroom and down the hall toward Séverine's bedroom, but this was finally too much of a violation for me. I was risking more and more with every passing moment, and I grabbed Giselle by the arms and stopped her.

"Do you have any idea what we're doing?" I said.

She reached between my legs and squeezed the eager hardness she found waiting for her there. "Give me a chance and I'll show you."

I took her hand and led her back into the living room. We sat down on the day-bed and looked into one another's eyes, as if awaiting a judgment from some wiser third party. She leaned forward, hesitantly. When I did not pull away, she leaned in farther, and then she kissed me, slowly at first and then full, wet, sloppy kisses, while she unbuttoned my shirt. When she had stripped me from the waist up, she knelt down in front of me, unzipped my pants, and with an energy and attention to detail that defied her exhausted condition, she demonstrated that she did indeed have an idea what we were doing.

By the time she climbed on top of me on the day-bed, the rarefied world of fine art, the danger of crossing Nazi collaborators, and even Séverine herself seemed a whole world away.

* * * * *

We lay on the day-bed for a long while, drifting in and out of sleep, a decorative throw wrapped around us. I knew that Séverine would be busy all day with the fashion show, that she wouldn't be home until late that night, but this did not keep me from falling into the grip of guilt and remorse.

The French do not think of sex the way Americans do, and though I'd been raised as American as they come, I had lived in Paris long enough to feel, if not comfortable with, then at least not entirely foreign to French mores. For the French, it is not necessarily the end of the world if your spouse or lover has an affair, and Séverine and I had both had affairs during the course of our eight years together. Because I was gone for such long periods of time, with so much uncertainty surrounding my work, our relationship faced more than the usual challenges to fidelity. However, when either of us had strayed in the past, it had always been when I was in some godforsaken Timbuktu for months on end, and it had always been brief flings with people we did not know in common. Sleeping with Giselle, on Séverine's own day-bed—this was unknown and dangerous territory. Considering Giselle's emotional state, I hardly thought I could depend on her for discretion, but I did not have the luxury of dwelling on this subject at the moment. We had done what we had done, and the consequences, if there were going to be any, would await us later.

I slipped out from under Giselle and left her sleeping, while I got dressed and found Séverine's *L'Indispensable* guide to Paris. I located the Quai Fernand Saguet, where Jean-Pierre had told me Benoît had gone the night before, but it was not in Paris: it was in Maison-Alfort, a suburb southeast of the city, and it wasn't on the Seine at all, but on the Marne, just above the confluence of the two rivers. Maison-Alfort was not exactly far away—its streets flowed seamlessly into the streets of Paris—but I had never been there before, and I didn't like the odds of showing up and just finding a particular barge. *Péniches* are constantly moving up and down the rivers of France, and a barge at that quay in Maison-Alfort last night could be all the way up to Chalon-en-Champagne on the Marne by now, or all the way down to Rouen on the Seine. Still, that was where the trail ended, so I figured that was where I had to pick it up.

My head was pounding. I took some aspirin and boiled water for coffee, then pressed myself an extra-strong cup before returning to Giselle. I sat on the edge of the day-bed and stroked her cheek with the backs of my fingers until she woke up. She blinked sleepily at me, her face now less drawn with panic but weary just the same. Her hair was a bird's nest of tousles and tangles.

"I'm going to go," I said.

"Where?"

"Try to find Benoît and the painting."

"And what will you do if you find them?"

"Benoît, I'll him leave to his own devices. The painting. . . well, I guess I'll bring the painting back to you. What do you intend to do?"

She yawned and stretched her arms, so that the decorative throw slipped down, exposing one breast. She watched me appreciating her body.

"I don't know," she said. "My black market contact has disappeared. The Count wants to kill me, I guess. The whole thing's botched."

"You think you could find someone else to buy the painting?"

"I don't know. I left my Palm Pilot and cell phone in my car, so I don't have my files with me."

"You mean whoever has your car also has your phone and electronic organizer?" I exclaimed. "With all of your personal information in it?"

"I'm afraid so. All my personal numbers, my business contacts, my schedule."

I sighed. "And those were the guys who beat me up?"

"No, the person who has my car—that was someone else."

"But he was driving a cream-colored Citroën?"

"No, I just stole that car. It was just lucky."

"Great."

"You know," Giselle said, "I have all that information backed up on my laptop, at the antique shop." She took my hand and put it over her breast, and I felt her nipple swelling and hardening. "All my contacts, I mean. You could bring it to me, if you want, and we could still try to sell the painting. Together."

My blood ran cold. For the first time, I felt that Giselle might not be merely confused and out of control, but that she could be malicious in the service of her goals. She had already turned on Séverine in a very tangible way—we both had. I was unsure where her allegiances lay or what new and dangerous ideas her ill-planned schemes might now suggest to her, and now I had compromised myself with her. Until this afternoon, my relationship with Séverine had never seemed more solid, and I was not given to casual sexual dalliances, and yet here Giselle lay in front of me, naked, inviting me into an increasingly complex web of deception, as her partner. For some reason, the invitation was compelling, and I kissed her and she responded eagerly.

"First things first," I said. "Let's see if we can actually find the painting."

I told her that she was not to leave Séverine's apartment, under any circumstances. Since she no longer had her cell phone, we would have to communicate through Séverine's home line, but I asked her not to pick up unless she used Séverine's answering machine to screen the calls and she knew for certain that it was me.

Giselle assured me that she would stay put. She said she would call the manager in her apartment building and tell him to let me in when I arrived, and she told me where I could find the spare keys to her antique shop, and where she kept the laptop in her office.

"And bring me some clothes from my apartment, would you? I'm not sure Séverine would be happy, if she knew I was taking her things."

She delivered this last line with collusive irony, as she stroked my cheek. I felt my stomach sink. I had no idea what I was getting into, but I was certainly getting into it.

6

The Worst Art Heist in History

I took Giselle's stolen Citroën and headed for Maison-Alfort. If the police were looking for the car, this immediately made me a target, but I assumed I was a target of one kind or another anyway, and there was a chance that the police at least wouldn't beat me up.

I crossed the Seine at Pont de la Tournelle amid a cloud of black smoke from the Citroën's noisy exhaust pipe. I tried to picture the scene in which Giselle had been forced to swap her sporty little BMW for this bucket of bolts. She must have done it right after she'd called me at the Orsay, since she'd had her cell phone up until then—I couldn't quite make sense of her story, and I thought it probable that she was hiding more from me than this one significant detail. I fought the car into second gear as I turned onto Quai Saint Bernard.

In most cities, traffic is based on a fluid system model, in which streets are like riverbeds and cars act like water flowing through them. In Paris, traffic is based on a particle physics model, in which streets trace the irregular paths of protons and electrons and cars bounce around each other in a dance of repulsion and attraction. Avenues dart off at thirty-five degree angles, come unexpectedly to dead-ends and change names in the middle of blocks, so that it's never clear exactly where you are or which direction you're headed, and French driving schools instill a Napoleon complex in their students—by the time Parisians get their licenses, every one of them honestly believes that he or she owns the entire system of roads from

Moscow to Madrid.

As I piloted the belching Citroën southeast along the Seine, half a dozen motorscooters swarmed around me, sliding with impunity in and out of my lane, sometimes within an inch of my bumper, their whirring engines emitting the high-pitched whine of electric weed trimmers. A man in a purple Peugeot cut me off and stopped suddenly in the middle of the block, so that I had to swerve violently to miss him, and then he flipped me off as I lurched by. At Place Valhubert, a pedestrian was crossing against the light, and when I decided to gun the engine instead of stopping for him, the Citroën stalled and an ancient Mini Cooper clipped my bumper as it veered around me; the driver then hit the wayward pedestrian's swinging plastic grocery bag, precipitating a shower of fresh cherries across my windshield. The pedestrian scurried to the sidewalk, and I reached out the driver's side window to snag a cherry from my windshield wiper. When I spit the pit out the window, it hit a motorcyclist, who appeared out of nowhere right beside me, and if he hadn't been talking on his cell phone at the time, I'm sure he would have spit right back at me.

After twenty minutes of such carnival stunt driving along the quay, I crossed the Seine again at Pont National and eventually came to the confluence of the Seine and the Marne. I parked the car on a street above the quay (that is to say, I abandoned it), wiped away my fingerprints and then crossed the Marne on a footbridge.

Looking back at Paris, down the Marne from Alfort, the city seems much more industrial than it does from the old downtown *quartiers* around the Marais. At the confluence of the Seine and the Marne, the Parisian suburbs are lined with shipping warehouses, smokestacks spewing black and white smoke, and quays lined with oil-streaked barges. Downtown, I can participate in the Paris of my medieval fantasies, but on the periphery there is only concrete and steel.

Quai Fernand Saguet was a narrow street that followed the Marne along the south side of the river. A mixture of modern apartment buildings and shipping offices looked out onto the water, and steps leading away from the street took me down to a landscaped promenade at the river's edge. The City of Maison-Alfort had spent considerable effort trying to beautify its riverbanks, and though the landscaped swatches of grass and flowers bordering the promenade were attractive, the grunginess of the docks themselves overwhelmed this meager prettiness. Aging black *péniches* were moored in a long line to heavy bollards set in a stone pitching on the banks, and the water around the barges was festering with Styrofoam trash, flotsam, and fetid masses of vegetation washed downstream and caught against the moored hulls. The smell of algae and urine swamped the pier, and I was thankful for the fresh breeze blowing down the Marne, which helped carry away the unpleasant odors.

I strolled along Quai Fernand Saguet, reading the names of the *péniches*, but there was no *Fascinage*. A few bargees, men and women both, were leisurely going about their business, hanging laundry on clotheslines strung across decks, sitting in lounge chairs chatting, smoking and reading newspapers. There were no permanent piers built from the banks into the water, so there was no way to approach a barge casually: to get to a particular *péniche*, you had to cross that boat's own gangplanks, so that, with your first step off the quay, you were already trespassing, and none of the barges looked hospitable to strangers. Bargees are notoriously disenchanted and disillusioned, possessed of a maverick *méfiance*—distrust of the government and most of its subjects.

I selected a barge at random to start with, the *Mirabelle*. It was painted a deep velvety crimson, and an unshaven man in a bright yellow fishing hat was hanging laundry on the deck, a cigarette dangling from his lips.

"Pardon me," I said. "Do you know where I could find Benoît Vicaut?"

He continued hanging laundry, without even acknowledging my presence. I waited while a shirt and a pair of trousers were clipped to the line, and then repeated my question.

He took a long drag on his cigarette and blew smoke. "Who wants to know?"

"I'm a friend of his. Luke Johnson."

"Johnson, eh? *Americain*?"

He went back to hanging his laundry, and I waited for what seemed a geological epoch, during which the bargee apparently forgot that I existed. Deciding to press my case, I stepped onto the *Mirabelle*'s gangplank, and quick as lightning the bargee flicked his cigarette at me and rushed over.

"Get the fuck off my boat!"

I stepped back onto the riverbank. The man stared fiercely. Perfect, I thought, I'm going to have a pissing contest with every bargeman along the quay.

I moved on to the next barge, where a man and a woman were sitting together on a metal ledge outside the pilot's cabin. The man was smoking a clay pipe and the woman was smoking a cigar. They seemed a little more relaxed than the first guy, and I repeated my query.

"Vicaut?" the man said. "Never heard of him. What's his boat's name?"

"*Le Fascinage.*"

"Never heard of that, either. Why you lookin' for him?"

"He's an old friend. He sent word that he was going to be in town and I should look him up at this quay."

"You might ask the lock-keeper," the woman said. She jerked her head toward the east, upriver. "He usually knows who's coming and going."

I looked up the Marne to the lock she had indicated, not far above the quay. The lock-keeper's station was on the other side of the river, across an arched pedestrian bridge. I thanked the couple and headed toward it.

Just below the pedestrian bridge, a grizzled old-timer was fishing in a deep pool, where water spilled out from the lock. Though the surface of the Marne appeared less dirty than the Seine, I wondered what toxic filth from far upriver was hiding in this pool and what monstrously deformed fish might come out of it.

"Anything biting?" I asked.

He shrugged his shoulders. "*Comme toujours.*"

I crossed the footbridge. Through the slats between the bridge's wooden planks, I could see water plunging over the spillway, directly below, and the soothing soughing of the roiling river echoed off the bridge. At the far side, I passed over a *péniche* in the lock chamber, as it was slowly raised for its voyage up the Marne.

All around the lock-keeper's office were signs forbidding entry to unauthorized personnel. There seemed, in fact, no permissible way to reach the lock-keeper at all, so I ignored the signs, opened a blue steel gate and walked across a short quay to the office. I knocked on the door and received no answer, so I tried the handle. It was unlocked, and I let myself in.

A clean-shaven young blonde man glanced at me, with no expression on his face. He was sitting at a broad black electronic board, whose controls I couldn't see. I looked over my shoulder at the lock, and waited for the young man to open the gates on the chamber so that the *péniche* could pass through. The barge captain's voice came through the radio, and they exchanged pleasantries for a moment, and then the lock-keeper fiddled with some controls and the lock gates began closing again.

Finally, the young guy appraised me while lighting a cigarette. Between Jean-Pierre and these smoking river rats, the tobacco industry would never go out of business.

"I assume you can read," he said, "so your stupidity can't be attributed entirely to ignorance."

"I'm looking for a barge called *Le Fascinage*. It's urgent that I find it."

"What's that to me? You know the penalty for breaking into a dikereeve's station?"

"I hardly broke in. The door was open."

"You *are* stupid, aren't you?"

What was it about riverboats that gave everyone around them Humphrey Bogart fantasies? "I'm going to be straight with you, all right?" I said, in my most ingratiating manner. "I need your help. A friend of mine's mother is dying, and it's important that I find him and bring him to the hospital. He's on *Le Fascinage*, so could you please just tell me if that boat has passed through here in the last day. He may never see his mother again."

The lock-keeper smoked at me unhappily for a moment, and then yielded. "I've never heard of it. What's your friend's name?"

"Benoît."

"Never heard of him, either."

"Could you radio some of the other locks, or some of the barges, and just put the word out?"

"I can't find a boat that doesn't exist," he said indignantly.

"The fact that you've never heard of it doesn't mean it doesn't exist." This was going nowhere. "Here's my card. If you see *Le Fascinage*, please call me. There's fifty in it for you if you do, and a hundred if you can keep the boat in the lock till I get here."

The lock-keeper took the card. I left his office certain that I would never hear from him.

* * * * *

There were a dozen little quays with barges docked at them within walking distance of the lock, and I walked up and down all of them. The bargees were uniformly unfriendly, unseemly, and more paranoid than the *Confédération Générale du Travail*. If any of them knew a barge called *Fascinage*, they weren't talking. Several people did admit to knowing Benoît and even spoke of him with fondness, but they had not seen him in the last twenty-four hours and didn't know where he was now. I left messages with all of them, without any real hope of finding either Benoît or the painting.

As I walked back down the Marne, I put myself in Benoît's shoes: if I were drunk and had a stolen painting stuffed into my coveralls, what would I do? The police had taken him to this quay, and he must have been along the river somewhere since then, since Jean-Pierre had received a message from a dock worker. Perhaps *Le Fascinage* was a garbage barge—as an unemployed garbage collector, Benoît would be familiar with refuse, so maybe the city dumps would be a good place to look.

I had no good ideas. I climbed the first set of stairs that led away from the docks and back onto the streets of Alfort and started looking for a metro stop.

* * * * *

By the time I reached Giselle's apartment, it was after eleven o'clock in the evening. The torpid sun had finally set for the night, and the last lingering glimmers of daylight were disappearing from the sky, promising a few hours' relief from the sweltering summer heat.

Giselle lives in a crooked, gabled building whose windows are protected by wooden shutters painted an absurdly bright orange. I believe the avant-garde color choice was influenced by the Pompidou Center a few blocks away, but the particular shade of electric pumpkin slathered over Giselle's building does not speak well of modernity.

The apartment manager let me in, and I was shocked to discover that Giselle's apartment had not been ransacked. It was just as neat and orderly as I had once imagined Giselle herself to be, and I wondered how international art thieves with such poor priorities could ever succeed: Giselle's apartment would have been my second stop, right after I ransacked her antique shop. Perhaps Giselle had formed alliances among the black marketeers that she wasn't telling me about. I kicked myself for failing to turn the screws on her a little, failing to make her divulge what had happened to her BMW and her electronic organizer.

I found Giselle's spare keys where she said they would be, then I dialed Séverine's home number and waited for the answering machine to pick up. "Hello," I said, "it's Luke, if you're there, pick up. Hello, are you there?" Giselle did not answer. I hung up and used my cell phone to dial Séverine's cell and got her voice mail—she was probably in a torturous meeting at some club on the Champs-Elysées, with a fashion designer screeching the merits of twill.

I reached Jean-Pierre at the Elephant: he had decided to keep the bar closed until order could be restored, so he'd had nothing to do all day but wait. He hadn't heard from the police, the thugs, Benoît or Giselle—he'd spent the day chain-smoking and playing solitaire.

"If this is what it's like being an international smuggler," he said, "I'd rather be a bartender. This is just too boring."

I agreed and told him about my long, fruitless search for Benoît along the quays of Maison-Alfort. In my job as a war photographer, I was used to this sort of thing: often during pitched confrontations, there will be many hours of sitting and waiting, then sudden, frightening bursts of activity in which people kill each other, and then many more hours of sitting and waiting or marching somewhere else to wait. I advised him to remain vigilant, since the brief eruptions of action would be critical and unpredictable. I told him, too, that Giselle might have left her secret hiding spot, since I could not reach her there, and that she might appear at L'Elephant Heureux.

"I'm beginning to think it doesn't matter what we do," I said. "All this foolishness will amount to exactly nothing if Benoît panicked and ditched the painting in a garbage barge. Or if the black market guys got to him first."

"It will probably amount to nothing, anyway," Jean-Pierre said. "Most things do." He hung up.

I went into Giselle's closet to get her some clean clothes and found myself appraising her wardrobe in a surprisingly voyeuristic fashion. I looked at her linen-blend dresses and silk blouses and conservative business skirts and imagined how her body would look draped in them, how her body would look slipping out of them. The act of opening the drawers of her antique dresser was unexpectedly tantalizing, and I selected undergarments that were anything but conservative, thinking of them caressing her curves, clinging to her supple skin. The hidden, troubled Giselle had found my secret weak spot, the evolutionary frailty of all men: she was the damsel in distress. How could we not rescue her? I folded a set of clothes into the most androgynous-looking shoulder bag I could find and then dialed Séverine's home number again.

"It's Luke again," I said into the machine. "Please pick up

and tell me you're there." I blathered into the machine for a minute and a half, hoping Giselle had merely fallen asleep and that my prattling would wake her, but if she was still at Séverine's apartment, she didn't answer the phone.

This was turning into the worst art heist in smuggling history. No one knew where anyone else was, no one knew where the art was, and I was about to walk into the Paris night carrying a woman's shoulder bag. Even a shootout, I thought, would be better than this, forgetting, as usual, that you must always be careful what you wish for, since you might get it.

7

Count Dumesnil

A light mist began falling as I walked toward the river. The uncertain clouds that had been building all evening had finally coalesced into a pleasant, cool night rain, and the streetlights were shrouded in thin, rainbow-sheened halos, making the avenues seem dreamy and ethereally soft after the harshness of the summer sun. As I passed Les Halles, the street became crowded with lollygagging tourists, and I had to dip and dodge my way around large groups loitering between the famous monuments of Paris. Rain usually chases tourists indoors, but now the saturated air felt like a relaxing exhalation, and some American schoolkids were dancing down the street warbling "Singin' in the Rain." The museums were long since closed for the evening, but the cafes surrounding Les Halles offered covered patios from which to observe the shimmering wet streets, and the crowds I pushed through would return home and tell stories of the romantic Paris rain.

I approached the Seine and kept my eyes peeled for shady black market types or Nazi collaborator types or any types at all, but no one seemed to be following me. Perhaps the Count had somehow caught up to Benoît already, taken the painting, and the drama was over, leaving me and those thugs to run around chasing each other for nothing. This possibility reminded me of the Battle of New Orleans, the unnecessary postscript to the War of 1812, in which British and American troops had fought each other more than two weeks after formal hostilities had ceased: no one could reach the garrisons stationed on the far frontiers quickly enough to tell them that the war was over, so they had continued fighting, and I felt a lot like those unwitting soldiers now, far from the action, still awaiting word, still ready to fight whether there was anything left to fight for or not.

I crossed the Seine on the Pont des Arts. Giselle's shop is several blocks above the river, nestled into a neighborhood of pricey specialty stores in Faubourg Saint-Germain. The shops and cafes here serve the gentry that Proust satirized, who retire to their private gardens at night to lacerate each other with telling comments—no tourists or rowdy French party-hoppers haunt these streets. As I hurried past one darkened art gallery and antiquarian shop after another, the meager pedestrian traffic fell away, and by the time I turned onto rue de l'Echaude—a narrow, medieval side street—I was completely alone.

My footsteps echoed across wet cobblestones. An uncanny shiver ran up my spine. For the first time since I'd become involved with this painting, I felt a genuine rush of fear. The total emptiness of the street was not merely peculiar but menacing: there were enough stark shadows along the facades of the ancient buildings, in doorways and recessed alcoves, that a person could melt into the darkness and never be seen. I stopped and waited for the reverberations of my footfalls to die away. No one else appeared. The only sounds were the distant white noise of traffic and the gently insistent susurrations of misting rain.

I laughed ruefully at myself, standing statue still in the rain, scaring myself with shadows. I was on a wild goose chase for a woman I should have been running away from, fast, and it was impossible to tell what unexpected danger lay around which dark corner.

Giselle was the one who was supposed to be having a crisis of values, but now I was unsure what I valued or where my priorities lay. Why was I throwing my lot in with Giselle? Because we had slept together once, under the worst possible circumstances? Séverine was so loving and reliable, so caring and predictable that I had begun to take her love for granted, and I wondered if, in the secret recesses of my heart, I was as conflicted about the value of love as Giselle was about the value of objects. In the same moment that I sensed real danger around me for the first time, I also felt the real possibility of losing Séverine, and I didn't know which I was more afraid of or why those feelings were so closely bound together.

Giselle's shop, D'Hier à Demain, looked just as it always did from the outside: no broken windows, no trenchcoat-wearing toughs loitering on the threshold. I let myself in and turned on the lights, and everything inside appeared well-ordered as well, straight rows of furniture, neat aisles of vases and crystals, a gang of chandeliers hanging in symmetrical diamond patterns from the ceiling. I held my breath a moment and listened, but the increasingly earnest rain against the windows dampened all other sound.

I set Giselle's shoulder bag on a table and threaded my way back to her office. Here, unmistakably, something was out of place: Giselle's usual compulsive ordering of every little thing had been upset—the office *appeared* perfectly neat, but I had seen Giselle straighten up at the end of the day, and little details now were wrong. Notepads were not lined up perfectly parallel to one another perpendicular to the edge of the desk at two millimeter intervals; a valuation guide had been pulled out from its shelf and not realigned with the others; and Giselle's chair had been pushed exactly square under the desk, where she would normally set it at a forty-five degree angle to the door. Someone had taken great care to make it appear that they hadn't been in the office, but no one could duplicate Giselle's precise, idiosyncratic neatness. I checked the hidden rollout drawer in Giselle's desk, where she kept her laptop computer, and found that the computer was missing.

Things were going from bad to worse: not only did I not know where the painting was, but now whoever was chasing Giselle had her laptop, with all of her records and files, and her Palm Pilot containing her complete rolodex as well. And they could enter her shop at will.

The longer I stayed there, in fact, the more distinctly I felt that I was being watched. I turned out the office lights, quickly checked the shop for intruders, and then switched off the shop lights as well. I grabbed the shoulder bag with Giselle's clothes and locked the door behind me as I stepped out into the street.

Rain was falling heavily now, and my shirt pasted itself to my skin. The street seemed as empty as it had when I'd first approached—and yet, the feeling that I was being watched grew stronger.

I hurried down to boulevard Saint-Germain, usually one of the busiest streets on the Left Bank, but even here traffic was clearing as the storm worsened. I searched the rain-drenched faces of everyone I passed and turned constantly to check for pursuers, but the people running at me from behind were just ducking into apartment buildings or rushing into the metro to escape the downpour. Still, the sensation of dread remained.

I've mentioned before that I'm extremely lucky, and this is how my luck often works, not by leading me in a perfectly straight line to my goals, but by suggesting, through hints, alarms and intuitions, what I shouldn't do in a bad situation. In times of crisis, people often get themselves killed by not listening to their animal instincts.

I glanced around again and noticed for the first time a figure in a long gray raincoat. Though I hadn't spotted the man before, he was little more than a block behind me, walking just faster than I was, as if trying to catch up. I quickened my pace. The man in the raincoat quickened his pace.

I turned on boulevard Saint-Michel, but found only half a dozen other pedestrians still on the sidewalks, scurrying for shelter. Car traffic had thinned as well, and now the gutters along the streets were running with dirty rainwater. I hurried toward the river.

I couldn't go to Séverine's or Giselle's or the Elephant or anywhere else if I was being trailed by black marketeers—the only place I could go was to the police, and that seemed less and less attractive. The million euros that Danton had mentioned were weighing on my mind. At that moment, I seemed about as far away from a million euros as I could get, but I had held the painting in my hands just the night before, and the freedom it promised called to me.

I dialed Jean-Pierre at the Elephant and told him that I was being shadowed. "Any suggestions?"

I could see him in my mind's eye taking a drag on a Gitane—he must have chain-smoked a whole pack since I'd spoken to him last. "What are you doing, Luke?" he said. "You've got to go to the police. Right now. Somebody's going to get hurt, really hurt."

"I've already considered that possibility. What I need is an *original* idea."

"I don't want to read your name in the obituaries tomorrow, my friend."

I told him not to worry, that I'd call back as soon as I got to safety. A gust of wind kicked up, blowing heavy splatters of rain across my face.

As I approached the Quai des Grands Augustins, the man in the gray raincoat drew closer. Though his gait seemed labored, he kept gaining ground. If this man had been staking out D'Hier à Demain, if he was the same one I had intuitively felt watching me, then he could easily believe that I had just picked up the painting from the shop—he could think that I was carrying it in Giselle's rather bulky shoulder bag. I quickened my pace again, until I was almost jogging.

I crossed the southern channel of the Seine on the Saint-Michel Bridge and reached the Île de la Cité. Just ahead of me, the Conciergerie loomed—the giant Gothic prison that had held Marie-Antoinette before her beheading. It was now a complex of courts and judge's offices—there were always *gendarmes* in front of the Conciergerie. I thought about what Jean-Pierre had said: all I had to do was march up to the police and I would be safe. But then I would have to spill the whole story, and I wasn't ready to give up on the Luce just yet. Or on Giselle.

I turned onto the Quai des Orfèvres, which traces a curving path along the south side of the island. I hugged the stone wall overlooking the river, glancing behind me to keep tabs on my unknown foe, and I realized that we were now completely alone on the quay. A blast of wind swirled cool rain all around me. The man broke into a run, and I put my head down and bolted.

At a full sprint, I was easily quicker and beat him to the Pont Neuf by a wide margin. His gait was gawky and stiff, and I suddenly recognized his labored movements as the clumsy exertions of an older man unused to exercise—the Count!

I ran onto the Pont Neuf and was just considering whirling to confront the old man when I heard the first shot. The ricochet sounded almost simultaneously as the bullet glanced off a stone bulwark behind me. I ducked my head and scampered in a weaving pattern across the street—an old and useful habit.

I reached the far side of the road and looked for an escape

route. If I crossed the bridge either way I was an open target. Stone steps to my left led down toward a dock at the western end of the island, but once you reached the edge of the river, there was no escape—the dock ended in a stone piling.

A second shot reported and I heard the bullet whine past my ear, much too close for comfort. There was only one way out.

I jumped onto the stone decking along the walkway and without hesitating threw myself off the bridge. As I plummeted toward the Seine, I flung Giselle's shoulder bag as far away from me as I could and then plunged into the surprisingly cool river.

The water was dark and dank, and I could feel little things brushing against my skin as soon as I splashed down—I couldn't tell if they were living or dead, fish, or just bits of industrial debris suspended in the mucky grime. As my descent through the water lost its momentum, my foot touched something soft. Thinking it was the bottom of the river, I tried to push off, but as soon as I did, the soft thing moved. I was so startled that I breathed water and kicked the thing as I tried to get away from it, paddling madly. The thing smacked against my leg, and I felt my lungs screaming with pain as they tried to expel the Seine through my mouth and nose.

I struggled toward the surface. The thing continued smacking at my leg, and then it grabbed me! Whatever I had kicked was now trying to drag me down into the river. I kicked the thing harder with my free foot and it let go.

When I finally gained the surface, I choked and spluttered for breath. Before I could get my bearings, shots rang out. I had hoped to swim some distance from the Pont Neuf underwater, to get out of range of the Count; instead, I hadn't even reached the western tip of the island. I was merely a few meters downstream from the bridge. Luckily, I was quite a distance below street level so I made a poor target in the dark, but whatever was in the Seine with me now had hold of my ankle again and was dragging me under.

I gulped a quick breath and then Paris disappeared above a murk of gloomy water, and I went down. I kicked and thrashed and got free, trying all the while to get downstream to avoid the Count's gunshots. I resurfaced and felt a weight push right up against me and then something hard drubbed me twice in the head, without much force.

"What the fuck!" I screamed.

A long moment passed. Heavy raindrops made the surface of the river dance, refracting light from the street lamps above in dizzying patterns. Finally, a voice croaked, "Luke?"

I was so surprised that I nearly went under again. "Benoît?" A shot rang out, then another. "Down!"

We dived together and swam as hard as we could downstream, coming up as seldom as possible for little gulps of air before diving again. By the time we stopped to rest, my heart was beating like a twelve-piece steel drum band, and I spun around to get my bearings. We were beyond the Pont des Arts, the first bridge downstream from the Île de la Cité. We took cover behind one of its abutments and looked each other in the face.

"What the hell are you doing?" I cried.

"I throw myself into the Seine *every* Friday night," Benoît said, matter-of-factly. "What the hell are *you* doing?"

"Somebody's trying to kill me."

"So I gathered." Benoît held up his left arm. There was a hole in his skinsuit and a large gash in his side, just below his armpit. One of the Count's bullets had grazed him, and he was bleeding into the water.

"We've gotta get downstream," I said. "Can you still swim?"

"Do I have a choice?"

As usual, Benoît had perceived the full breadth of his alternatives in a moment. We swam.

8

Le Fascinage

By the time we reached the Pont de l'Alma, it was clear that the Count wasn't dogging us from the shores. I assumed he had gone after Giselle's shoulder bag, and for the moment we seemed safe.

We dragged ourselves out of the river, Benoît laboring and pale. The gash in his side was superficial but long and still bleeding, and the Seine is not exactly the Fountain of Youth. I shuddered to think what nightmarish microbes had already found their way into Benoît's bloodstream.

I wrung out my shirt and gave it to him as a bandage. As he stanched the bleeding, he remained composed and even philosophical—he didn't even seem angry that the Count had just shot him, and we sat on the stone promenade on the bank for a while, panting. The rain had gradually slackened to a steady drizzle, and the relative freshness of the rainwater felt good after the Seine.

"We've gotta get you to a hospital."

"Doctors!" Benoît spat. "Arrogant bastards!"

"Maybe, but they have this magic potion called penicillin."

I helped him apply pressure to his wound until it stopped bleeding completely, and I noticed in the meantime what a mess we were. I had kicked off my shoes during our swim, and one of my socks had been swallowed by the river, and now my shirt was mottled with Benoît's blood. The bullet hole in Benoît's skinsuit had torn and grown larger, and in addition to the nasty looking gash, you could also see the top of his rotund belly peeking through.

I pulled out my cell phone, but the river had done it in. There was no way to reach Giselle or Jean-Pierre right away—but I had the most important piece to the puzzle sitting right beside me.

"So where did you stash the painting?" I said.

"Under the *fascinage* along Quai Fernand Saguet. Didn't you get my message?"

"Yeah, but I spent half the day down there and nobody ever heard of it."

"Heard of what?"

"*Le Fascinage.*"

"What are you talking about?"

"There's no such barge, Benoît—at least, not at that quay."

Benoît shook his head. "It's not the name of a barge. It's a bundle of sticks!"

He then explained the meaning of the word *fascinage* in French: it was a bundle of wooden staves or posts tied together. He hadn't given us the name of a barge at all—he'd told us to look for a literal bundle of sticks!

Despite the fact that I've lived in Paris for more than ten years and can often pass for a Frenchman in everyday conversation, there are still occasional words and usages that trip me up. I had never even heard the word *fascinage* before and couldn't imagine why there was a need for it—a bundle of sticks! I consoled myself with the fact that Jean-Pierre seemed just as mystified by the word as I was and figured it must be part of the bargeman's argot.

"But I still don't understand. You hid the painting under a bundle of sticks? Just out in the open?"

"Not out in the open. The *fascinage* is floating in the water near the docks, and the painting is suspended in the water below it."

I flopped back on the stone walkway and groaned. "You dumped it in the Seine?" So much for the million euros: we had nearly gotten ourselves killed for a waterlogged piece of canvas floating in the river, a former masterpiece that was now worth exactly nothing.

"Of course not," Benoît said. "You think I'm an idiot?" Benoît then described the canister into which he'd rolled the painting and the way he'd water-sealed it before dropping it into the river. "Bargees hide things in the river all the time. You know, art thieves aren't the only ones who smuggle things."

I could have kissed him. "Well, let's go get it!"

Benoît sighed. "If it's all the same to you, we can get it in the morning. It's not going anywhere, and if we don't have it, no one can steal it from us." Now it was his turn to lie back against the stones. "Besides, I'm not used to getting shot—it takes something out of you."

"We need to take you to the hospital."

"If I'm still conscious, I'm not going to the hospital."

"All right. Let's go to the Elephant, then. Jean-Pierre may not have penicillin, but he stocks plenty of painkillers, and we can rest there till we figure out what to do."

* * * * *

We caught the last subway of the night toward the Marais. Even in the freak show of the late night metro, Benoît and I called attention to ourselves. Once we got away from the Seine, it became apparent that the stench of the river was clinging to us, and the fact that we were half naked and Benoît was wounded made us easily the most intriguing people on the train that night. Even the girl with pink pubic hair wearing a see-through dress was no competition.

We got out at the Bastille stop. The drizzle continued and even the usually hectic Place de la Bastille was quiet, with only a few taxi drivers sitting in their cars smoking, and the cafe patios all empty and beading raindrops. The relative calm of the city was a relief, and for the time being no one was chasing us, shooting at us or beating us; when Jean-Pierre let us into the Elephant, I let my guard down for the first time all day. The three of us, at least, were together again.

"Whew," Jean-Pierre held his nose when we walked in. "You guys smell like rotten fish."

"Rotten fish should be so lucky," Benoît said.

Jean-Pierre's eyebrows rose when he saw the gash in Benoît's side. He locked the doors behind us, and Benoît fell into an easy chair at the back of the bar. Beyond Jean-Pierre's concern, I could see him silently calculating the cost of re-covering the chair, but instead of telling Benoît to move, he said, "Let me get a clean towel for that cut."

"It's not a cut, it's a bullet wound," I said.

Jean-Pierre stared at me. "I told you someone was going to get hurt."

"It's not so bad," Benoît said, but Benoît had definitely looked better.

I picked up the phone and dialed my own mobile number, then entered the code to get my voice mail. Séverine had left half a dozen increasingly worried messages, and Giselle had left a single vexed message wondering why I hadn't returned to Séverine's apartment. I then retrieved the messages from my home machine and found more worried calls from Séverine, and a message from Joseph Danton at the Orsay Museum. He said he had spoken to some people at the Ministry of Culture and could guarantee a reward for the return of the Luce, though he didn't say what the reward would be. I listened to one of Séverine's messages a second time and cringed with guilt at the loving concern in her voice. I was glad that she was safe, and I told myself that I wished she were with me, so I could take her in my arms; but as soon as I wished that, I longed for Giselle instead. It was a confusion I didn't need at that moment.

Meanwhile, Jean-Pierre had cut away the top half of Benoît's skinsuit and was cleaning his wound as delicately and thoroughly as any nurse could. "Séverine has called quite a few times," Jean-Pierre said. "You should let her know what's going on."

I dialed Séverine's mobile number and she picked up right away. "Are you all right?" she said. "I've been worried sick."

"It's been some day," I hedged. "Where are you?"

"In a taxi heading for my shop. The first collection premieres tomorrow night, so I've been making a million last minute adjustments."

"You mean you haven't been home?"

"No."

"And you still have more work to do tonight?"

"No, I'm just dropping some things off, then I was going to come to your apartment."

I told her we were all at the Elephant and that she should come there instead. She agreed and we hung up.

"Séverine's on her way," I told Jean-Pierre. "I think we should all sit down and decide what to do next. More than that, there's strength in numbers."

"Giselle should be here, too," said Jean-Pierre. "If this is anyone's problem, it's Giselle's."

"But who knows where she'll turn up next or what she'll do. She certainly isn't where I left her this afternoon." I found a bottle of armagnac and three glasses behind the bar and brought them to Benoît and Jean-Pierre.

"I suppose we'll have to decide for her, then," Jean-Pierre

said.

I poured us all double shots. Benoît drank his right down and waved his glass for a refill. Jean-Pierre stood up and threw the towel he had used to clean Benoît's wound into a rag bin behind the bar.

"Before Séverine gets here," Jean-Pierre said gravely, "may I make a suggestion?" Benoît and I looked up. "Maybe you should go home and change? You two really stink."

* * * * *

Benoît and I made a quick dash to my apartment, and you could have knocked me over with a feather when Giselle greeted us at the door. Not only was I surprised to see her there, but I couldn't believe what she was wearing.

She had on a blood red, off-the-shoulder 1920s-style shimmy dress with batwing sleeves—a dress I recognized as one of Séverine's prizes from last summer. Dozens of tiny faux diamonds sparkled in the netted chiffon overlay, and Giselle had even taken the trouble of finding a perfectly matched diamond-and-ruby necklace from Séverine's jewelry hutch. I couldn't believe how audacious she had been in selecting this outfit: not only had she made herself a beacon for anyone following her, but Séverine would not be the least bit happy to see her in it, especially since Giselle had finished the ensemble with Séverine's silver Vera Wang slingbacks. Giselle had swiped one of the sexiest dresses in Séverine's wardrobe and then *accessorized*.

Because Giselle is a little taller than Séverine, the already short dress rode even higher above her knee, and I was struck not only by Giselle's sang-froid in wearing it, but by how perfectly the color of the dress complemented the creamy pale skin of Giselle's thighs, in a way it had never exactly suited

Séverine's more olive complexion.

"Where the hell have you been?" I said. "I thought you'd been kidnapped or beaten up or something."

"You were gone *all day*. It's not like I could just sit there and wait for Séverine to come home." She gave me a significant look that Benoît noticed.

"But you don't mind rifling Séverine's closet." I pointed at her necklace.

"You were the one who suggested I find something of hers to wear."

"Yeah, a wrap or a muu-muu, not a sexy flapper dress."

"You think it's sexy?"

Benoît rolled his eyes and pushed his big bare belly between us. "Séverine's going to kill both of you," he said. "Let's remember why we're here."

"How did you get in?" I asked.

"The landlady knows me well enough."

Benoît stripped out of his tattered skinsuit right in front of us, and Giselle noticed his bullet wound for the first time. The awful smell of our clothes and our bedraggled appearance finally impressed her as well.

"What—?"

Benoît went into the bathroom to shower, while I gave Giselle a quick redux of our adventures with the Count. She turned suddenly somber and harassed again, and her forehead creased into a deep frown. I told her that we were going back to the Elephant to meet Jean-Pierre and Séverine, and I suggested that she change into a pair of my trousers and a t-shirt.

"Why? You don't think they'd like the way I look?"

"Isn't it bad enough, the trouble you're in? Why do you want more trouble?"

"You think Séverine is trouble?"

"No, I think you're trouble."

"But you love trouble, don't you, Luke?"

"Jesus," I said. I was liking the old, conservative, uptight Giselle more and more.

After Benoît had showered, I searched my medicine cabinet and found some old tincture of iodine, which I applied to his wound. It wasn't antibiotic, but it was something. Then I dressed the wound with some gauze left over from a nasty cut I had gotten on some razor wire outside of Rangoon.

Benoît is a couple of sizes larger than me, but he managed to squeeze into a pair of my old gym shorts, whose elastic waist had long since given out. Then I found one of Séverine's sleep shirts in my closet: it was just loose enough to stretch over Benoît's belly, though it unfortunately had a picture of a children's cartoon giraffe on the front. The get-up made Benoît look like a sad velvet clown painting come to life.

I showered quickly and changed and was just about to insist that Giselle put different clothes on, but then I thought it might work out for the best this way. Would Séverine be more suspicious of our tryst if Giselle showed up in the flapper dress or in a pair of my old blue jeans? With the dress, at least, Séverine's wrath might be directed more exclusively at Giselle, and it might not occur to her that Giselle had been naked in front of me.

I wondered how the civil war in Chad was going, and not for the first or the last time decided I would be better off there, hiding behind my camera.

9

A Conspiracy of Thieves

On our short walk back to the Elephant, I persuaded Giselle to at least remove Séverine's necklace, the most flamboyant and presumptuous part of the outfit, and I slipped it into my pants pocket. Séverine was already there when we got back, sipping a glass of white wine at the bar, and when she saw Benoît and Giselle, fourteen different shades of shock, outrage and confusion crossed her face.

"The prodigal daughter returns at last," Jean-Pierre said to Giselle. He kissed her on both cheeks and then turned to me. "Where did you find her?"

"She found us," I said quickly.

"Why the hell is everyone wearing my clothes?" Séverine exclaimed.

"Would you rather see us naked?" Giselle asked. She glanced at me indiscreetly, and I felt like crawling into a hole.

"I'm sorry, Séverine," said Benoît. The cartoon giraffe on Séverine's nightshirt distended and stretched with each breath he took. "We really had no choice."

"No choice?" Séverine looked at Giselle evilly as Giselle sauntered by, flaunting the flapper dress.

"There wasn't much in your closet that would fit me," Giselle said.

"What were you doing in my closet?"

"Luke's place wasn't safe."

Giselle took the bottle of armagnac on the bar and poured herself a glass. She raised it to her lips and drank, looking all the while at Séverine. Séverine knew full well that Giselle never drank armagnac and that I always did, and this gesture of complicity gave me a presentiment of doom that the worst guerrilla ambush never had.

The look on Séverine's face when she turned to me was wounded and furious, and my throat tightened. "It's not as bad as it sounds," I said. "It's just that the Count was trying to kill us."

"The Count?" she cried. "What Count? How is *that* better than it sounds?"

"Let's just slow down, okay?" I asked Jean-Pierre to pour me a white wine, Séverine's drink of choice, and I flashed Giselle a warning look. "Séverine, I'm sorry we used your apartment without permission. I had to think of a place to hide Giselle, because it wasn't safe for her to be walking the streets. The dress she'll have to explain herself."

Séverine looked to Giselle for an explanation, but Giselle just held my gaze and said nothing. My staring at Giselle suddenly seemed a clearer giveaway than anything Giselle might say, so I turned back to Séverine.

"Benoît is wearing your nightshirt," I continued, "because we had to jump into the Seine to get away from Count Dumesnil, and his other clothes were ruined. I didn't have anything else to fit him at my apartment."

"Who the hell is Count Dumesnil?" Séverine said.

"That's why we're all here right now," I said, as soothingly as I could. "So we'll all know what's going on and we can decide what to do calmly."

"That's not why I'm here," said Séverine.

I spread my arms in a supplicating gesture. "We have some decisions to make tonight, decisions that will affect all of us, so please—"

"I don't see what there is to decide," said Séverine, addressing me alone. "Giselle's the problem—and now people are trying to kill you and Benoît? We have to get rid of that painting. That's all there is to it."

"There really is more to it than that," I said. I walked over to Séverine and put my hand on her arm, in a gesture that I hoped would be reassuring. I looked into her eyes, and after a long moment she softened somewhat—against her will—and I knew that she would at least hear the story.

"How's your head?" she asked. She stroked my cheek.

"Not bad, all things considered."

She ran her fingers through my hair and rubbed my head, then sighed and looked away, until her eyes fell on Giselle again. "I don't see how this can be good."

"I agree with Séverine," Jean-Pierre said. "That painting has been nothing but trouble, and the best thing to do is turn it over to the police and get it off our hands." He took a drink of armagnac. "However, I do believe it's important for all of us to hear the whole story." Always the peacemaker, Jean-Pierre. "We should talk about it and agree."

Séverine stared out the window. Benoît took the bottle of armagnac to a table usually reserved for playing backgammon and chess and sat down in one of the armchairs. Giselle, for once, just stood and waited.

"Whatever else you think of it," I told Séverine, "it's a pretty good story."

"Like when that sniper killed your driver in Bosnia?" Hard anger flashed across her face, but then yielded to simple irritation. "Fine." She got up from the bar, took a seat next to Benoît, and looked sadly at her giraffe nightshirt, now completely ruined.

Giselle took the seat directly opposite Séverine and crossed her legs theatrically as she sat down, showing more thigh than a chorus girl at the Moulin Rouge. Jean-Pierre looked at me shrewdly, as if to say, "There are times when it's better to say no."

* * * * *

Jean-Pierre assumed control of our impromptu meeting, and the fireworks between Giselle and Séverine took a momentary back seat to questions of art, thievery, money, Vichy collaboration and how we'd all gotten into this mess. Séverine, Jean-Pierre and Benoît heard the whole story for the first time, and Giselle learned the details of what had happened to the painting after she'd given it to me, and how the Count had tried to kill Benoît and me.

While Giselle was telling her tale, she became somber. Though she had come into the Happy Elephant this evening looking for a fight with Séverine, she soon became supplicating and depressed. There were no sly suggestions, double entendres or thinly veiled digs in her story, and I was moved again by her inner torment and her foolish financial choices. Even Séverine, it seemed to me, tempered her judgment somewhat when Giselle described how she had voluntarily gone bankrupt because of her conflicted feelings about the value of beauty, how romantically and hopelessly she loved the beautiful things that passed through her shop. Though Séverine never expressed feelings like this in her own work with gorgeous models and ravishing clothes, I imagined that Giselle's sentiments struck a chord with her—that she at least understood Giselle's misgivings.

Almost everything in Giselle's double life was now exposed, but I noted that her account had omitted the loss of her BMW, not to mention the hijacked Citroën, so that I wondered exactly what she was hiding and why. She also failed to mention that we had become lovers, so I felt that I could not ask about the BMW, lest she expose our tryst, and Giselle's covert looks told me plainly that we were now collaborating in each other's lies, weaving a secret relationship of our own right in front of Séverine. I felt heroically foolish.

By the time Giselle had finished her story, we were well into our bottles of wine and armagnac, and it was nearing three o'clock in the morning. Jean-Pierre stood up and stretched.

"So now there's still the question of what to do," he said. "I *am* moved by the dire state of your finances, Giselle, and I understand how you might justify stealing from a Vichy collaborator, but I still say no amount of money is worth this risk. Benoît and Luke could have been killed tonight. Dead. This Nazi needs to be brought to justice for everything he's done—and there are other ways to avoid bankruptcy than stealing."

"You might not say that if you saw my books," Giselle said.

"Maybe you shouldn't be in this business in the first place," I said, "if you have such clouded feelings about it."

"No. I think I understand now a little better about the value of things. Something about dealing with the Count, and these creeps from the black market, has really opened my eyes. It's made me realize very clearly how important the money really is. And look at what I'm doing now—I didn't steal that painting for the love of art or for the beauty of the tableau or for justice. I stole it for *money*, the same reason anyone else steals. I guess I had to hit the bottom of the spiral before I saw just how twisted my attitude about beauty really was. I was just too sentimental."

"Be that as it may," Séverine said, "we're still talking about attempted murder, theft, the black market and Nazi collaborators. If we go to the police now, they may not even charge you with a crime, especially not when you turn over the Count *and* the painting and all the other stolen artifacts in his castle. You could come out of this looking like a hero."

Giselle snorted. "I don't want to be a hero, I just want to have my life back the way it was. I think you'd see that a little clearer if you were losing *your* shop. If you were losing something *you* loved." She looked at me.

Séverine raised an eyebrow. "But I'm not, am I?" She looked back and forth between me and Giselle, finally settling an imperious, withering look on Giselle.

The rest of us were too tired to rise to the energy of this exchange, and even Giselle seemed to regret it, as she shriveled back into her seat. I reached past Séverine for the wine bottle and poured myself another glass.

"My two cents' worth?" I said. "We sell it. None of us will ever get a look at a million euros again. Nobody will miss the painting except the Count—it's already been missing to the world for two generations—and he's about as dirty as dirty can get, anyway. He's a war criminal, or his mother was and he's done nothing to correct the crimes, so I won't shed any tears for his loss. Giselle may have gotten us into this for bad reasons, but we're into it, and I don't think right and wrong are so clear in this case."

"When did stealing develop a gray area for you?" Séverine said. "Besides, exactly who would you sell the painting to? Giselle's black market guy is missing and the only other people you've met have beaten you up and shot at you. Why are we even talking about this?"

"What about this Joseph Danton?" Jean-Pierre said. "He said there's a reward. Maybe it would be substantial enough for Giselle to keep her business. Then, everybody would win."

This suggestion struck me as so eminently reasonable that I wondered why it hadn't been obvious to everyone all along. But then Benoît, who had been quiet the whole time, spoke up with a force that caught us off guard.

"Giselle isn't the only one who needs money. There's a million euros on the table, and we're going to settle for some government handshake?"

"Is there really a million euros in the offing?" I said. "How much was your black market guy going to pay?"

"Nine hundred thousand," said Giselle. "I guess some guy in Osaka agreed to buy it for a million and a half."

"Okay," Benoît said. "So maybe we could even find that Japanese guy and get the million and a half ourselves. I mean, the Ministry of Culture?" He snorted. "How much would they give us? Besides, even if a finder's fee saved Giselle's ass—they could give her a Medal of Honor, for all I care—what would *we* get out of it? We've risked everything for this goddamn painting and for what? I just got shot! I want my share."

Benoît almost never speaks of money—he'd never given any indication that he cared about it one way or another. He scrapes by on unemployment benefits and can afford to drink at the Elephant only because Jean-Pierre likes him and gives him his drinks at cost. Benoît presents himself as a vagabond scholar of the Seine who has no interest in anything but the river.

"What would you do with that much money, Benoît?" I said. "You wouldn't know what to do with two hundred euros, much less two hundred thousand."

"You're right about that," Benoît said. "Two hundred isn't worth getting out of bed for. But with two hundred thousand— or a hundred and eighty thousand, or however much it turns out to be—I could buy my own *péniche*. I could be a riverboat captain on the Seine!" He said this like a little boy inventing a magical land, and the whole room lit up with Benoît's dream. "I could be a real bargeman!"

"That's nice, Benoît," Séverine said dismissively. "But you still don't have a buyer. Who is this Japanese guy? What happened to the original black market contact? And beyond that, it's illegal even to have the painting, and you could get yourself killed or arrested trying to sell it."

"Could you get another buyer?" I asked Giselle.

"I know lots of people with lots of contacts, and I have a good enough reputation. I'm sure I could get someone to lend me their rolodex, if I told them I'd been robbed. From there, it's just lots of phone calls and a little luck."

"How long did it take to set up the first sale?"

"Less than a week."

Jean-Pierre spoke up. "I'd like to point out that the results of that first sale weren't even mixed. Giselle lost the painting, Luke got knocked unconscious, my bar was broken into, and Benoît got shot. There was, in fact, never even a moment when the exchange of money might have happened, and there's still the Count to consider, even if you manage to sell it. He won't be happy no matter what, and he's already proven he's willing to kill you."

"Obviously, there will be risks," Benoît said. "But there have already been risks, and we have nothing to show for them."

"In for a centime, in for a euro?" Séverine scoffed.

"The only thing I've ever really loved is the Seine. If I were a barge captain, I could be with her all the time. And I might remind you all," he said, "that I'm the only one who knows where the painting is."

"That's it," Séverine said. She stood up. "I want no part of this gang of thieves." She turned to Benoît. "I'm ashamed of you, Benoît. You're the most peaceful soul I know, and here you are trying to hold something over your friends' heads like you're some Pigalle thug." She turned and headed for the door. "Luke, I'm meeting a designer from Fendi in my shop at eight. That gives me about four hours' sleep."

She unlocked the door and strode out of the Elephant. By

that, she meant that I should catch up with her by the time she found a taxi or our relationship was over.

"So you're out?" Jean-Pierre said.

"When do you want to get the painting?" I asked Benoît.

"First light."

"Wait till eight. I'll meet you here." Benoît nodded, and I turned to Giselle. "You can find a buyer?"

"I'll try."

"What about you?" I asked Jean-Pierre.

"I don't think so. I mean," he shrugged his shoulders, "I guess you can still spend your money at my bar, wherever you get it. But I just want to run my little place. I don't want trouble."

"All right, then, it's settled."

"Not quite," Jean-Pierre said, nodding toward the street and Séverine.

I rushed out the door and ran down rue des Tournelles. I caught Séverine at the Place de la Bastille, just as she was flinging open the door of a cab.

10

Pour l'Amour ou l'Argent?

Séverine and I passed a difficult night at her apartment, neither of us sleeping much. Séverine complained that I never knew what was good for me. It was one thing, she said, to go off to other people's wars and risk my neck—there might even be something noble in *that*—but it was a different thing entirely to court death on the streets of Paris over a painting.

"It's almost like you want to die," she said, sitting up in bed next to me. "Like you don't know how to live unless somebody's shooting at you. Isn't it bad enough that I worry about you constantly while you're away, but now I have to be terrified that somebody will kill you right in your own apartment? Or in mine?"

She was as fed up with me as she'd ever been, and it didn't help that this was happening during haute couture week, her busiest time of the year. She felt that I was sabotaging her work with my international smuggling fantasies.

"It's no fantasy of mine," I protested. "Half the time, I don't even know what's going on. You heard Giselle's story."

"Yeah, I've heard enough of Giselle's story. If she had problems, she could have come to any one of us for help, but this. . . and the way she was looking at you tonight. She's completely out of control."

It occurred to me, as she said this, that Séverine herself always needed to be in control, and maybe that was why Giselle and Séverine had always liked each other. Though Séverine gave the appearance of being quite easygoing, in her business she was just as regimented, obsessive and severe as Giselle had once seemed to be, and in her private life she loved order above all else. Séverine's trade as a hat designer required her to be whimsical and inventive, but she channeled all of her frivolity into her creations: the money side of her business was flawlessly pragmatic, and her personal life was calm, highly structured and predictable.

It was this very predictability that had always comforted me in our relationship: after the death-defying risks of my work, I knew that I could depend on Séverine for her tranquility and composure, and the time I spent in Paris was relaxing because Séverine allowed me to take her for granted. To the extent that we could be domestic together, she was happy, since she organized our domesticity, and I had thought I was happy with that arrangement, too.

"Can you imagine how much damage she's done to herself?" Séverine continued. "She's ruined her business over nothing, and it's not like she'll have many friends left when this is all said and done. Even in the best case—if she turns the Count over, collects a reward and gets off scot free—nobody will want to do business with her again. Nobody will trust her with their family's private things. Everybody has something to hide."

"Not everybody was a Vichy collaborator."

"No, but everybody has love affairs, everyone has secrets, and you're not going to invite someone like that into your home, someone who may turn your secrets over to the government, who may print them in the papers. She's ruined, whether she saves her business now or not—it will only be a matter of time."

It seemed by her tone that Séverine was taking pleasure in Giselle's downfall. I wished I could have defended Giselle in some way, but I could sense by the tension in Séverine's body that my sympathies for Giselle would not be tolerated, and a false word now might expose the whole affair. I couldn't tell whether Séverine suspected that Giselle and I had slept together or not, but the fact that I had risked so much for Giselle already was a bad enough betrayal in Séverine's eyes, and there was no way I could defend such recklessness with appeals to Giselle's friendship. My only defense was my own love of danger, a defense that Séverine had provided me.

At the same time, I wished that I could join Séverine in her condemnation of Giselle, that I could take pleasure in the fact that my girlfriend would never self-destruct in such a manner, that my girlfriend was lying beside me now as loving and stable as ever, and that I need not involve myself with the black market or Nazi Counts any more. If I wanted to, I could simply lie in Séverine's arms and forget about Giselle's inner torment and wrecked life, because even if Séverine knew that something had happened between Giselle and me, she made it clear by her tone and in her body language that I was safe with her and could remain with her as long as I pleased. But Giselle's demons now seemed the most erotic thing I had ever known, and I was drawn to Giselle even though she was certainly keeping secrets from me, even though she was willing to hurt me, maybe maliciously, and even though stability and calm were the last things she could offer.

"Just promise me this, Luke," Séverine said. "I'm going to take a holiday when fashion week is over. Stay out of trouble until then, don't take any newspaper assignments, and then come away with me. We can go to New Zealand or Tahiti, some place far away where they're not killing each other, all right? Just the two of us."

I promised. I promised a whole host of things as we drifted off to sleep, and it seemed that I might even be able to keep those promises: stay away from the Luce, stay away

from Giselle, then go away with Séverine to an island para-
dise, and keep the old way of life that Séverine and I had carefully constructed for ourselves. What could be easier? I still
loved the feel of Séverine's body—her chest rising and falling
softly against mine, her nose snuggled into my neck—but I
was no longer sure I loved her pragmatism, which had kept me
grounded for so long. What was this sudden longing for excitement, when my life was filled to overflowing with excitement
already? The life Séverine always invited me toward—a life of
fashion journalism instead of war photography, of the absurdity of couture instead of the fervor of violence—seemed, for
those moony moments that we lay together waiting for sleep, a
truly sensible life, with stability and love and even a family one
day. But my heart refused to be sensible, and at the moment
it was beating for Giselle, for the dark soul Giselle had always
hidden beneath her prim business suits, for the smell and taste
of Giselle's body.

Séverine stirred against me. "Luke?"

"Mm?"

"*Je t'aime.*"

"I love you, too, Séverine. I love you, too."

* * * * *

After I escorted Séverine to her shop the next morning, I
made a bee line for the Happy Elephant. The day was cloudy
and milky gray but the rain had blown over. The streets were
once again alive with shouts and car honks, and the sidewalks
were teeming with arguing people and squealing children and
busking street musicians.

At the Elephant, Giselle let me inside the bar and indicated the sleeping mass of Benoît sprawled across an easy chair.
Jean-Pierre was nowhere to be seen.

Giselle looked like the ragged end of nowhere: her wan complexion, frizzy hair and haggard eyes made the gay colors of Séverine's flapper dress almost grotesque. The way the dress rode so high up her thigh, which had seemed devastatingly sexy the previous evening, now seemed merely lurid and revealing. I made a mental note never to sleep in evening wear.

"I told Benoît I'd wake him as soon as you arrived," Giselle whispered. "But I want to talk to you first."

She pulled me into a little alcove, two steps higher than the main floor, where a couple of small private tables hid from view. She scooted her chair close to me.

"I think I can find a buyer for the painting," she said, "but I'm not sure I can get a very high price on such short notice, and I wasn't planning on splitting the money three ways. There's going to be a lot less in the pot than I'd imagined."

She sighed and looked at me nervously, as if working up the courage to ask a difficult question. I was sure, in fact, that she was going to suggest I give her my share of the loot, that she was going to play on my sympathies or even blackmail me by threatening to tell Séverine what had happened between us. Given her dangerous unpredictability, I was ready for almost any new scheme that somehow risked my life and benefited her—any new scheme, that is, except the one she finally proposed.

"There's no way I can save my shop for less than half a million. I have almost no merchandise left, I don't have enough steady business to carry me, and I have significant debts."

I was aghast. "You're telling me half a million just gets you *even*?"

"I'm not operating some chintzy knick-knack shop, Luke. I figure I need that much to get the business back to the shape my mother left it in—half a million and two years of real work, and even then some exceptional finds, which you can never

106

take for granted. My shop was so successful because my family worked constantly for three generations building and improving it, ninety years of good luck and good sense and savoir-faire. No amount of money can buy that kind of time and dedication, and that's why it's worth saving.

"However," she continued, "I was thinking last night about something you said before you left. You said that maybe I shouldn't be in this business, if I have such mixed feelings about it. Remember? And I said, no, I understand about the money now, and I love my shop, and I've been clinging to the shop all along, because it's the only thing I've ever known. But I've been up all night thinking about it, and I think you're right."

"You mean, now you've decided to give up the shop?"

"Not exactly. But I still feel mixed up about everything, and I'm not sure I want to work as hard as all that to reestablish the clientele—who's to say that I wouldn't fall right back into the same perverse pattern and just wreck the business again? Besides, truth be told, I hate rich people, and I've been thinking of better ways to spend the money we could make from the painting."

"Like what?"

"Like starting over—I mean really starting over, some other way. I could liquidate the shop and settle my accounts and still have enough money to make a fresh start, almost anywhere."

"But. . . I don't understand. You could have done that right from the beginning, without all this drama and danger. You've risked everything expressly so you could hang onto your old life, and now you just want to drop it?"

"I was desperate, Luke, and I didn't know what to do. I wasn't thinking clearly."

"Well, if you want to liquidate and quit, you could certainly do that without selling the painting. Why don't we just turn it over to the police and get out of this trouble, if that's the case?"

"No, it would be a total disaster without the extra money to pay off my debts," she said. "I'd be left with less than nothing. Besides, there's Benoît to consider... Anyway, after yesterday, I had another idea—what if we took the money left over and went somewhere, somewhere completely different, and started a new life?"

"We?"

She took my hand. "You and me. You've been all over the world, you surely know a place where that money would last, where no one would ask any questions. We'd have time to build a life together."

I looked into Giselle's bloodshot eyes with utter disbelief. Putting aside for the moment that I had no idea whether she could be trusted an inch, whether she even knew what she wanted any more, I had just promised Séverine that very morning that I would go away with *her*!

Giselle was close to tears as she awaited my reaction. I tried to imagine disappearing with her to a Caribbean pirate hideout, where we'd live happily ever after on our ill-gotten gains, but this was the least likely scenario yet. And yet... I wondered who Giselle really was, after all, which pole of her personality was closer to the truth, and who she might become once this crisis had passed; and I wondered if my attraction to her was simply my need to be needed. Séverine, like the Giselle I had always known, was incredibly self-sufficient, and I thought my new-found affection for Giselle might really be a fondness for my own gallantry. I wasn't attracted to Giselle because she was out of control, I told myself—it was because she needed me to be in control for her, and I liked feeling responsible for someone else in a way that was at once practical and dramatic. It was surely momentary, and when the crisis passed, my feelings of love would pass as well.

"Giselle." I squeezed her hand. "When we made love yesterday, don't you think that was just another expression of the craziness happening all around you? Don't you think it was just fear and relief and a whole bunch of things all mixed up together? We've never even flirted with each other before."

Giselle shrugged. "You've always been with Séverine, or half a world away in some revolution. I've always been maintaining appearances, even with you guys at the Elephant." She wiped her eyes with the back of her hand. "There are lots of things I've done and felt in secret over the years, that I've never told anyone. Lots." She caressed my cheek, then leaned forward and kissed me lightly on the lips. "When things went wrong with the black market guy, when I was in real trouble, why do you think I came to you?"

"You didn't come to me. You came to the Elephant. I just happened to be here."

"I came here looking for you. I knew you'd be here."

Well, I thought, that's one way to know you're a regular. Benoît was stirring on the other side of the room, and I held Giselle's gaze for just a moment longer. I thought of Séverine in her shop a couple of kilometers away, diligently pleasing some fashion fop from the house of Fendi.

"Just think about it," Giselle said. "I'd really love to be with you."

She started to get up, but I grabbed her wrist. Benoît groaned and sat up, rubbing his eyes.

"What happened to your car, Giselle?" I hissed.

"It's a long story, Luke," she whispered. "It's not that important." She kissed the tips of her fingers and then touched them to my forehead. "Honestly."

One of the many valuable things I've learned listening to

journalists interview people is that when someone says 'honestly,' they're lying. She got up to wish Benoît a good morning and make us all some espresso. I followed her out of the alcove. Benoît looked particularly bad and groaned heavily as he stood up.

* * * * *

We needed to replace Giselle's and my cell phones, and we had to find presentable clothing for Benoît and Giselle before we could do anything. We went upstairs to Jean-Pierre's apartment and woke him up: he gave Giselle his own mobile phone to use and loaned Benoît money for clothing. To my mind, he was just as implicated as the rest of us were in this criminal enterprise, since he continued to help us with our scheme even after he'd declared himself against it. I didn't understand why he remained reticent about accepting a cut of the money, but then, as Paul Valéry once observed, everybody has his reasons.

I sent Benoît to a clothing store I knew was open early, just north of the Place des Vosges. "Remember," I said before we split up, "Keep your head up. The Count is still out there somewhere, and those two meatheads who beat me up aren't what you'd call friendly."

"You don't have to remind me," Benoît said, pointing to a stain on Séverine's nightshirt, where some blood from his bullet wound had oozed through during the night. We arranged to meet at the Saint Antoine metro entrance at Place de la Bastille in half an hour.

Giselle and I went around the corner to my apartment, where I grabbed some cash from a secret pocket in my mattress (I'm old-fashioned that way). I then found some faded blue jeans and a plain pullover for Giselle. I held them out and motioned her toward the bathroom to change, but she slipped out of the flapper dress right then and there, in front of me. She was naked underneath. She opened one of my dresser drawers and helped herself to some boxer shorts, then she took her time unfolding the clothes, sizing them to her body, displaying herself fully for me before slowly stepping into my pants and slipping on my shirt. She spread her arms wide, asking with her eyes how I liked her in my clothes. I sighed: I thought she looked fabulous even gaunt and beleaguered, and I tried to forget that she was playing an angle on me and I didn't know what it was. She kissed me, and I just stood there for a while, letting her.

I excused myself and went into the bathroom to put on a fresh shirt and sports jacket. When I came out, Giselle wrapped her arms around me and stage-whispered a thank-you so treacly and maudlin that I felt embarrassed for both of us—for her that she could attempt a con so artless, and for me that I could fall for it anyway. She kissed me again, and I felt more confused about her than ever, and absolutely alive.

On the way back to the Place de la Bastille, I stopped at my cellular store on boulevard Beaumarchais and purchased a new mobile phone. Something about dealing with the shopkeeper seemed uncanny to me, and I became especially keen and alert again. When we left the store, I scanned the street for trouble. We couldn't have lost the thugs or the Count completely, and somebody out there already knew where we all lived, where we might be during the day and when we might be there. We seemed overdue, in fact, for some new calamity, but Beaumarchais was its usual bustling self, and if someone was following us, I didn't spot them. The uncertainty of this enterprise, the fact that we were targets out in the open with no clear idea who might come after us next, was fraying my nerves.

Benoît was already at the rendezvous spot when we arrived, wearing denim overalls and a forest green t-shirt—not far from his usual outfit. It *was* unusual, however, to see Benoît *himself* looking forest green, and I told him again that he should go to the hospital.

"I just need some more sleep," he said, "and I'll be fine. Let's sell this painting, so I can recuperate in peace."

Peace, though, seemed very far away. Even if we sold the painting, the Count was not going to be happy to lose a priceless treasure, and I thought the coming negotiations, the mutual blackmail and threats, would require delicate handling, indeed. It was possible that we might sell the painting and still have a volley of bullets to dodge.

We descended into the rush hour helter-skelter of the subway. Giselle headed for the number one line, toward the antique district where she would hopefully arrange a quick, illicit transaction; and Benoît and I went to number eight, toward Maison-Alfort, to collect the painting.

11

Criminal Logic

When we reached Alfort, Benoît led me to exactly the same quay I had started with the day before, where the barge-man from the *Mirabelle* had told me to get the fuck off of his boat. We walked a little downriver from the *Mirabelle*, until we came to a particularly fetid and disgusting pool of stagnant water behind a neglected, rusted-out *péniche*. On the water's surface, a thick green scum had accumulated, making the bundle of sticks floating in its midst look repulsive.

"*Voilà*," Benoît said. "*Le fascinage.*"

I couldn't believe it. I had stood fifty feet from the painting yesterday, but it had been impossible to tell that such an unwholesome mire of algae, muck and trash hid a fortune. For that matter, the *péniche* that loomed over the pool was in such a state of dilapidation that it could have passed for modern art.

Benoît's *fascinage* was floating about three and a half feet away from shore, just out of reach, where it scraped against the derelict barge's hull. Benoît skittered down to the water's edge with surprising agility, given his exceptional girth and his bullet wound. He grabbed what looked like a rotten wooden plank bobbing among the trash. Though it seemed to be just another piece of driftwood, the plank had been secretly tied to a stone on the quay with a length of invisible filament fishing line.

Benoît pulled the board out of the water and took it to the opposite end of the rusted-out *péniche*, where he used it as a gangplank to go aboard. Soon, he appeared on the deck of the barge with a steel hook tied to a heavy rope.

"You want to give me a hand?" he said.

I crossed the moldering, improvised gangplank, and with both of us guiding the hook, we snagged the *fascinage*. Once we'd hooked it, we hauled the bundle of sticks on board, and with it came a black tube, with two black metal clasps at one end. It was like a postal container for maps or blueprints, except that it was made of some light metal and was matte-painted, so that it could not reflect light. I wondered what the bargees normally smuggled in it—it was small enough that I supposed it had to be drugs or precious stones or illegal documents. At the many black market bazaars I had seen, I had never come across anything like it.

Benoît unfastened the tube's clasps, peeled away a tarred gasket seal from the inside rim, and removed the painting. We spread it out on the deck.

The colors looked incredibly vibrant in the pallid morning sunlight. From a foot away, though, the picture itself was unintelligible—it looked like nothing more than clumps of painted dots, which made your eyes go blurry when you stared at them. I held the painting up for Benoît, who stepped back a dozen feet. His face changed as he moved away, as the dots of color on the canvas coalesced into a scene of the Seine. I thought he was going to cry.

"I know that bend," he said. "Near Herblay, right? You can still see wildflowers there in the spring—it's very peaceful. . . and beautiful."

He appraised the painting a moment longer, then turned away to look out at the Marne flowing by, to fight back his tears. I rolled the canvas up and put it back in its tube. "Let's get going," I said.

We walked to the other end of the *péniche*, where I noticed that our soggy makeshift gangplank had disappeared. Benoît pulled at my shirt sleeve and pointed around the ship's fore bulwark. "*Merde*," he said.

"*Putain de merde*," I agreed.

Two men were staring at us from the bank, the same two guys who had jumped me the day before last at my apartment. The smaller of the two, the one who had worn the blue suit, who had decoyed me by scratching at my door and falling against it, was holding our gangplank.

Benoît sighed and gave me a world-weary look. "It had to happen eventually," he said. "But there are two of us and two of them, and we've got the painting. This time, I think, the odds are in our favor."

I thought it the wrong time to point out that, though we did indeed have the painting, we had no way of getting to shore with it under these circumstances; and though Benoît's math was technically correct, he hardly looked capable of putting up a fight. He was green! On the other hand, these two jokers couldn't use our slender gangplank to come aboard, since it would force them to cross one at a time; and since the boat's gently bobbing deck was two feet higher than the shore, it would be nearly impossible for them to jump on board without using the plank.

I looked up and down the quay—there was a single jogger running along Alfort's prettified riverbank promenade. A couple of fisherman were casting into the pool below the lock, and there were probably some bargemen on their *péniches* within shouting distance. The lock-keeper surely had a pair of binoculars that he could train on us in the event of a disturbance. It wasn't much traffic, but it was still a little too busy for the toughs to take out guns and shoot us just like that. As cocky as they appeared staring at us from the quay, it looked like we were going to have a Mexican standoff.

"Good morning, boys," the smaller man said. "I couldn't help noticing that you're holding our painting. Would you mind tossing it over to us?"

"Painting?" I said. I held up the tube. "This? No, no—this is just some *pain moulé et saucissons*. Maybe you'd like to come aboard for a picnic."

They sauntered to a point directly across from us and stopped. We stared at one another.

"Why do you want us to hurt you?" the larger man asked.

"You're really in no position to make threats," I said. I retrieved my cell phone and dialed Jean-Pierre's number. The smaller man dropped the gangplank and withdrew a gun from a shoulder holster under his sports jacket.

"I stand corrected," I said. I dropped the cell phone.

Benoît bowed at the waist in a very formal manner, then said, in an aristocratic tone I had never heard him use before, "Gentlemen, would you be ever so kind as to allow me to freshen up." Then he turned on his heel and strode away to the *péniche*'s captain's cabin, where he quickly descended out of sight.

I don't know who was more surprised by this maneuver, me or the thugs, but the thugs did nothing but look at one another. The one with the gun did not even raise it to threaten Benoît, and I took this as a sign that he was not really prepared to shoot us. Not yet, anyway.

"This is certainly awkward," I said.

"Just give us the fucking painting," the gunman said. He pointed his weapon at me.

I hefted the tube and wondered, if I threw it out into the Marne, if any of us would ever see it again. "Fine," I said. Hoping that Benoît was preparing a miracle below deck, I stalled for time by opening the clasps on the tube and removing the painting. "Let me hand it across to you." I held the canvas out, but it immediately wilted and drooped against the side of the ship.

"Put it back in the tube, you numbnuts," the larger man said.

"Right. Of course." I propped the tube up on the deck and held it between my legs, then slowly rolled the painting back up and pretended to have trouble making it fit into the mouth of the container.

"We can just shoot you and do that ourselves," the gunman said.

"Sorry."

I still did not believe he would fire the gun in broad daylight with so many potential witnesses, especially not with the logistical awkwardness that would follow: they would have to board the boat to get the painting after they shot me, which would take a moment, and then there would still be Benoît to deal with. For that matter, I didn't believe the gunman really wanted to shoot me, because I've seen that look before and this man didn't have it—but you never know. I slid the canvas back into the tube, adjusted the waterproofing gasket, and then fumbled with the first clasp. "It was easier to do this," I said, "when no one was threatening to kill me."

"Nevertheless," the gunman said, and then I heard a loud pop.

I flinched, and the air was split by a sharp whistling and then a sizzling sound very close to my ear, and the gunman cried out. I hit the deck already rolling, and when I found that I was unharmed, I jumped up again and ran to the other end of the *péniche*, shielded from the two thugs first by the starboard bulwarks and then the captain's cabin. Behind me, the thug with the gun was swearing and yelling incoherently. Benoît slid around the other side of the captain's cabin toward me, holding an empty flare gun.

"They're going to shoot us now, for sure," I said.

"Give me the painting." I handed Benoît the tube, and he secured the clasps. "You distract them," he said. "I'm going for help."

"Going where? Distract them how?"

Benoît grasped the tube tightly under his right arm, stood up, and took a running leap into the Marne. He emerged slightly upriver from the *péniche* and thrashed pathetically upstream. Between his bullet wound and the awkward shape of the metal tube, I was sure he would drown. I heard footsteps approaching across the deck, and I realized that the only sure way of distracting the thugs from Benoît was by making myself a target. I had spent my whole life trying to avoid being shot, and now I would have to invite it!

I stood up and ran around the far end of the captain's cabin. I nearly tripped over an old mop lying across the deck, and I picked it up to use as a weapon, though what I hoped to do with it against a gun, I'll never know. I saw the smaller man, the one with the gun, running along the shore, trying to get a clear shot at Benoît. Out of sight upstream, Benoît yelled something watery and incomprehensible, and the gunman leveled his gun and fired at the water. The shot reverberated loudly, and I looked up the quay to see if anyone had noticed, but at that moment, the larger of the thugs appeared around the cabin, swinging a black baton at my skull.

I fell backward on the deck and the baton whiffed over my head. On his backswing, he brought it down across my knee.

I let out a gargly groan and grasped the mop handle. As he lunged toward my head again, I stuck the mop head into his chest and he exhaled a surprised "oof" and staggered. I stood up, but as soon as I put weight on my injured knee, I fell to the deck again. There was no question of running now, so I wheeled the mop back and took a swing, but my attacker caught it by the head and ripped it from my hands. He threw it into the river.

I scuttled backward on the deck like a three-legged crab. "I don't have the painting," I said.

To show his recognition of this fact, he lurched at me and swung his baton again. I kicked him in the shin with my good leg. He lost his balance and fell forward and the baton crashed across my left arm, just above the elbow. I kicked again, aiming for his groin, but my foot bounced weakly off his thigh.

Up the quay, another shot rang out, and then I heard shouts. Someone yelled "Rémy."

My attacker recovered his balance and swung again. Lying on my back, with both feet in awkward positions, I couldn't dodge his blow. I averted my face and rolled, but the baton found the left side of my neck. I felt as if my windpipe were collapsing, and the world went completely purple, the color of pain and nausea.

I heard a voice that seemed tinny and very far away shout "Benoît!" I was sure I was going to vomit, but instead I felt a sharp rap to the side of my head and I blacked out.

* * * * *

When I woke up, I found myself lying on a ship's deck. I lifted my head and realized that there was a pillow beneath me, and when I looked around, I saw that the rusted out *péniche* had been replaced beneath me by a newer boat, painted a rich crimson. I sat up and found that I was on the *Mirabelle*.

The unshaven man in the bright yellow fishing hat, who had nearly attacked me when I'd set foot on his gangplank the day before, was sitting to my right, in a deck chair, smoking a cigarette. The yellow hat was now pulled down nearly over his eyes, so that his expression was hidden. Beside him, smoking a clay pipe, sat Benoît, in an entirely different but familiar set of clothes—his green City of Paris garbageman coveralls.

My head throbbed. I felt thin and empty. The sun shining through gray clouds overhead seemed like a dream sun, and the gentle bobbing of the boat made me want to throw up. I touched the top of my head, which was tender. I had trouble swallowing. I felt as if someone had driven a nail through my right knee. I let out a long sigh that unintentionally turned into a groan.

"Sleeping Beauty," the man in the yellow hat said, with a dismissive grunt.

"Fuck you, Prince Charming." My head was foggy, and I shook it to clear the cobwebs, but this only made jets of pain shoot all around my scalp into my neck. I noticed the black tube lying next to Benoît's deck chair. Then I saw that Benoît was holding a gun in his lap. "What happened?"

"Why don't you ask them?" Benoît said. He motioned toward the *Mirabelle*'s captain's cabin.

I struggled to my feet and limped heavily across the few steps to the cabin. Inside, tucked away from the view of passersby, our two attackers sat with duct tape over their mouths, their hands and feet secured with ropes. They looked at me with hatred.

I turned back to Benoît. "They don't want to talk," I said. I sat down near Benoît on a metal platform. Benoît introduced him as the *Mirabelle*'s captain, Rémy Regnault. "We've met," I said to Benoît. "I came here yesterday looking for you, and this guy threw his cigarette at me."

"And today," Regnault said, "you almost got me shot to return the favor. So let's call it even." He blew smoke at me as if he were a dragon blowing out a warning before he spewed fire.

"The good captain here saved our asses?"

Benoît explained that when he had dived overboard, his sole intent was to make it to the *Mirabelle*, since Regnault knew all about the Luce and was aware that there might be trouble. In fact, the black metal tube that now guarded the painting belonged to Regnault, and the captain was used to a certain amount of turmoil surrounding less than legitimate merchandise. Benoît had told him to be on the lookout for strangers prowling around the decrepit *péniche* next to his, and Regnault had been periodically checking the *fascinage*. When he heard Benoît's shouts and then a gunshot, he realized immediately what must be happening, and he slipped up from below decks and grabbed the Taser stun gun he kept in the *Mirabelle*'s cabin.

With the gunman's attention trained on Benoît, Regnault had surprised him and shot him with enough electricity to knock him on his back, unconscious. Benoît had then alerted Regnault to my plight. Regnault had relieved the unconscious gunman of his pistol and raced down to the rusted-out barge. He had used the pistol to persuade my attacker to take a calm stroll down to the *Mirabelle*, where Benoît and Regnault had bound and gagged the pair. They had then retrieved me from the other barge, carrying me here and laying me out to recover.

"How long have I been unconscious?"

"Couple hours."

"A couple of *hours*?" I exclaimed. "And you've just been sitting here smoking?"

"What were we supposed to do?" Benoît asked.

He had a point. "Were there any witnesses? No police, obviously, or we'd all be in a paddywagon."

Regnault scoffed. "River people don't call the police," he said. "The lock-keeper radioed, but I told him what was what. He's a good kid." I remembered the lock-keeper as an insolent, self-satisfied punk. "You owe him two hundred dollars," Regnault said.

It was unavoidable, I supposed, in a city this size, to do anything without a certain number of witnesses. We would have to count on the contrarian nature of the bargees and the profit motive of the lock-keeper to keep us out of prison. I wondered if Regnault would now want a share of the spoils.

"Have you heard from Giselle?" I asked Benoît.

"How would we have?"

"Has my cell phone rung?"

"No." Benoît looked around. "I guess it's still on the other barge."

I stared up into the cloudy sky for a long while and then down at the slow, brackish green river. Just upstream, a pleasure boat was being lowered in the lock. "And you haven't questioned our prisoners?"

"I decided to wait till you came around," said Benoît. "I thought they could use a little time to think about their position."

I nodded and looked into Benoît's eyes. For the first time, I recognized there a kind of indifference, a passive cruelty that I see often in the eyes of the teenage boys who kill each other in African villages. He had now been shot at twice, wounded once, and was turning progressively darker shades of green, until he almost matched the color of his beloved Seine. Séverine would certainly not recognize Benoît's "peaceful soul," as she had called it, if she could see him now.

I asked Regnault for something to drink, and he spat into the river, as if anything I might ask would be the most unreasonable thing he had ever heard. He got up and went below deck. When he returned, he gave me a plastic cup of whiskey. I had actually been hoping for water, but I drank down the hooch, then signaled Benoît that it was time to question our prisoners.

Regnault, Benoît and I crowded into the captain's cabin and stood over the two thugs. I ripped the duct tape off the mouth of the bigger guy, the one who had twice beaten me unconscious. I was impressed by the fact that he made no sound at all when the tape came off. I pressed the tape down onto his scalp and then ripped it off again, this time yanking some hair out by the roots, at which he conceded a grunt.

"Who the fuck are you guys?" I said.

"Who the fuck are *you* guys?" he snapped back immediately.

I turned to Benoît. "Do you think we should beat them first or burn their eyes with cigarettes?"

"I'd just wait till dark and drown them in the river," Regnault chimed in. "I've got some scrap iron we could use for ballast, then we could take their bodies downstream and dump them in the Atlantic. Very clean and neat."

"We can always do that later," Benoît said. "But for now, if we want them to talk, we'll have to hurt them."

"I don't know that we even have to hurt them, if they'll just cooperate," I said.

"This good cop, bad cop shit is for amateurs," our captive said with a sneer, at which Regnault kicked him viciously in the right armpit. He crumpled and fell over on his side, and I suddenly realized with great clarity that we were all in a lot of trouble, that all of our lives were growing permanently more dangerous and complicated with every moment.

Even if we managed to sell the painting, it would not be the end of this affair. These thugs would remember this treatment and come after us later, and it was too late to shake hands all around and call it quits now. Benoît knelt down and pushed the guy back upright.

"That was simple enough," I said to our captive. "How did

you feel about it?"

He did not answer, and I was reminded of a time when these same techniques had been applied on me in a jungle camp outside of Ahuachapan, El Salvador. I felt a wave of sympathy for the guy and would probably have become disgusted with myself if he hadn't just beaten me in the head with a baton. This, after all, was no helpless political pawn, no villager caught in the crossfire: he was a criminal who had twice attacked me violently, whose partner had shot at Benoît. But as I was justifying my actions to myself, I heard Séverine's voice in my head—when did beating people develop a gray area, she would say. Who made you the law to mete out punishment? I knew then in my gut that she was right, after all, about everything, that this was nothing but dangerous lunacy, but it was already too late.

Without warning, Regnault kicked the man again in his right armpit. He crumpled again and this time moaned pitifully.

"When somebody asks you a question," said Regnault, "you answer it."

Benoît pushed the guy upright again, and I knelt down to look him directly in the eye. "Why do you want us to hurt you?" I asked, mockingly repeating the question he had asked me when he'd first approached us at the other *péniche*.

"I don't," he said.

"Wasn't that easy?" Regnault said. He feinted a kick and the man flinched.

"Who are you guys?" I said.

"We work for Tristan Orliac. He sent us to pick up a painting from Giselle Mounier two days ago."

"By 'pick up,' do you mean 'steal' or 'buy?'"

"We were supposed to take it from her. Steal it."

"We need to call Giselle and check that," I told Benoît. "See if she knows this Orliac."

I limped out of the captain's cabin, off of the *Mirabelle*, and back to the nameless, decrepit barge where I had dropped my phone. Rémy had thoughtfully left the moldering gangplank in place, so I crossed, somewhat precariously, to the deck and found my phone, kicked up against a rusting jackstaff.

I dialed Jean-Pierre's mobile number, and Giselle answered on the first ring. "Have you ever heard of Tristan Orliac?" I asked.

There was a long pause. "Why do you want to know?"

"Those two goons who've been following us around work for him."

"They work for Tristan?" There was an even longer pause while she processed this information.

"Who is he?"

"He's my black market connection," she said. "He had set up the deal with the Japanese collector. I guess he double-crossed me."

"Looks that way. Looks like he never had any intention of paying you for the painting."

"How do you know about Tristan Orliac?"

"We've got his goons tied up on a boat in Alfort. We'll tell you all about it when we see you. Any progress on a new buyer? Someone—how can I say this without sounding ridiculous—someone a little more reputable, this time?"

"Not yet," she said. "I've got an idea, though."

I told her to call me as soon as she knew anything, and then I hung up and limped back to the *Mirabelle*. I found Benoît and Rémy as I'd left them, standing over the thugs, who looked as if they might have been beaten some more. I told them what I'd learned about Orliac and the potential new buyer.

"You probably shouldn't be talking so openly in front of these guys," Benoît said.

I shrugged. "Probably not." I was still preoccupied with what we would have to do with them once we sold the painting. Drown them to keep them quiet? Out of the question, of course. But what, then? What would prevent them from coming after us? Though Benoît seemed blasé about the thugs, I was beginning to think I'd have to go off to another war just to avoid getting killed.

My knee ached where the bigger guy had sapped me. I limped out of the cabin and back onto the deck. Benoît and Regnault taped the goon's mouth shut again and then joined me.

"Well," I said to Benoît, "what do you think?"

"Wait for Giselle."

"What about them?" I motioned toward the captain's cabin.

"We'll have to let 'em go once we sell the painting. I don't know. What difference does it make?"

"You don't think they'll want a piece of us?"

"It's not personal," said Benoît. "These black market deals don't always work out. Ask Regnault. That doesn't mean you kill whoever gets in your way. Maybe you take your revenge if they cross your path again, but I don't think they'll come after us." He shrugged. "They're just somebody's hired men, anyway."

I looked to Regnault for confirmation of this supposition, but he looked out at the river, poker-faced. "They've already tried to kill us twice," I said.

"No. They could have killed you in your apartment if they'd wanted to. They could have killed us both just now if they'd *really* wanted to—could have shot us the first moment they saw us. They just want the painting, that's all, and they want it because somebody else wants it. It's not personal," he repeated. Benoît sat down in a deck chair and closed his eyes.

He slumped, rubbing the bridge of his nose between his thumb and forefinger. He seemed deflated after this latest physical test. "I don't know how things work in those wars you photograph," he continued, "but this is just crime, not anarchy."

I sat down in the deck chair beside Benoît, leaving Regnault to stand. Regnault lit a cigarette.

"The only one who's really tried to kill us," Benoît said, "is the Count."

I thought this a preposterous assertion, though I agreed that we should still be concerned about the Count—his stake in the painting, in the potential loss of his reputation, made him more dangerous than any black market thugs. He had tailed me *himself* from Giselle's antique shop, after all, which underscored just how personally he took the matter: he had enough money to hire his dirty work done for him, but he had nevertheless gone to the trouble to shoot at us with his own hands. Moreover, there was no way the Count would be acting completely alone to retrieve the Luce, and it would now be obvious to anyone watching us on the Count's behalf that we were holding the painting right here on the *Mirabelle*—we had even, stupidly, unfurled the canvas in broad daylight on the other barge—and he would surely come after it. It seemed that we were incapable of acting with any discretion or cleverness.

My cell phone rang. It was Giselle.

"I've found a buyer."

"Excellent. Who, where, when, and how much?"

"We're selling it back to the Count, for half a million."

"What?!"

"We're going to make the exchange tonight, at the Opéra-Comique."

My heart sank. "Tell me you didn't do that, Giselle." The Opéra-Comique is one of the venues used for fashion shows during couture week, and it was obviously no coincidence that

Séverine would be working at the Opéra-Comique that very evening. "Do you *like* seeing me suffer?"

"*Au contraire, mon trésor,*" Giselle said. "Where can we meet?"

12

Giselle's Secret

I told Giselle to come to our quay, but she said that under no circumstances would she go anywhere near Tristan Orliac or his goons, now that she knew about the double-cross. She suggested that I come to D'Hier à Demain.

"We're easy targets hanging around your antique shop," I objected. "The Count will double-cross you, too, and we already know he can let himself in—you may not be safe there even now."

"And you feel safe standing guard over Orliac's men?"

"They're bound and gagged."

"Don't be a fool, Luke. Tristan will come after you there, mark my words. He knows by now that something went wrong."

I reluctantly agreed to meet Giselle in the most public and least dangerous place we could think of, the Luxembourg Gardens, where I hoped to convince her to change our rendezvous location with the Count. I was still conflicted about my feelings for Giselle and for Séverine, but I knew that if I entertained any hope at all of continuing my relationship with Séverine when this caper was finished, Giselle's flaunting of the heist at the Opéra-Comique would have to be averted. Séverine would never stand for it. Beyond that, I felt a stone in the pit of my stomach, as if some still unknown danger were close by, and I didn't like the fact that Giselle was still keeping secrets from me. We had the painting, and we had an agreement to exchange it for money, but that and two euros would buy me a cup of coffee.

Benoît was happy enough with Giselle's deal: his one-third share of half a million, just over 165,000 euros, would still be enough to buy a *péniche*, and with the art theft now effectively converted to a ransom scheme, he thought we could all relax. In Benoît's opinion, we could be reasonably certain that the Count would follow through on the deal, rather than risk more trouble.

"It's over," Benoît said. "All we have to do is make the drop at the Opéra-Comique tonight, slip away with the money, and that's the end of that. No more third parties, no more black market, no two-bit creeps with guns. We did it."

He sat back in his deck chair, his exhaustion suddenly turning to relief. Benoît rarely smiles, but now a big, broad grin crept across his face, and I could see by the sparkle in his eyes that he was picturing himself behind the captain's wheel of a barge, slowly pushing cargo up the Seine.

"The drop point will certainly have to change," I told Benoît. "The Opéra-Comique is too high profile in the first place, and I don't want Séverine involved. Besides, I don't trust the Count. I see no reason why Dumesnil would pay half a million euros for his own stolen property, if he can avoid it."

"He'll pay," Benoît said, "because if he doesn't we'll expose his whole illegal collection, and then he'll have nothing. Half a million is a drop in the bucket to guys like this, Luke—he owns a castle! Now, if you'll excuse me, I'm going to start outfitting my *péniche*." Benoît stretched out ostentatiously in his chair and closed his eyes, in a silent-movie pantomime of dreaming and planning.

I stood up and walked away, along the *Mirabelle*'s stern fender. My intuitions are not always accurate—I often go far out of my way to avoid situations that turn out to be harmless—but you can't trust your gut half the time: you have to live by it or not, and my gut was telling me that some new danger was closing in. There were enough obvious threats still looming that I didn't need to be psychic to worry, but I couldn't put my finger on the specific person or thing that was troubling me. I looked at Benoît, green but contented, and for the first time in my life I felt like smoking a cigarette myself.

A movement above the quay caught my eye. On the riverbank looking over the docks, on the little street fronting the Marne, a red BMW convertible glided silently into view.

"Benoît!"

I motioned emphatically. Benoît and Regnault clattered up next to me at the railing. The convertible stopped right above the *Mirabelle*.

"Not Giselle?" Benoît said.

I briefly recounted the part of Giselle's story that she had kept from our little group at the Elephant the previous night, the part about losing her car that she still had not completely explained to me. "I have no idea who it is," I said.

From our angle, the Z8's driver side window was a shiny black slate partially obscured by shrubbery at the top of the bank. We couldn't see in, but we made perfect body silhouettes for a practiced marksman, who might assassinate all three of us before we could even react to the first shot.

"Orliac?" Benoît said.

"Maybe."

Benoît pulled the revolver out of his coveralls pocket and cocked the hammer. "Let's split up." He nodded toward the dock, suggesting that we fan out and approach the car from different directions. The convertible's driver side door swung open.

A young woman stepped out. She was skinny, with long brown hair tousled around an elfin face. She wore an untucked navy blue blouse.

She cupped her hands and called down to us. "Luke Johnson!"

Benoît and Regnault looked at me. "I've never seen her before," I said. She motioned for me to come up the bank.

"A trap?" Benoît said.

"Make her come down here," Regnault suggested. "Who else might be waiting in the car, eh?"

"Let me have your gun," I told Benoît. He handed me the revolver, and I uncocked it and put it in the outside pocket of my sports coat.

I limped across the *Mirabelle*'s gangplank to the quay and followed the riverwalk to some concrete stairs set into the bank. My head was pounding once again from my second beating in forty-eight hours, and my knee throbbed. I leaned heavily on the railing as I climbed to street level. The young woman was waiting for me at the top of the stairs, her hand on her hip in an unassuming, almost relaxed posture.

She was even more diminutive up close than she'd seemed at a distance, but her small stature was more than compensated by the fierceness in her eyes, which were flecked silver-blue and gray, like pieces of crushed glass. She held out her hand forthrightly and I shook it while looking over her shoulder at Giselle's car. The little convertible held no passengers.

"I'm Manon Orliac," she said. Alarmed by the name, I let go of her hand and felt for the gun in my pocket. "I've c-come to see the p-painting."

I looked down at Benoît and Regnault, who were leaning on the railing of the *Mirabelle*, watching us expectantly. "You've come to see the painting?"

"That's right. D-d-didn't my mother tell you?"

"Your mother?"

"She said she'd t-t-telephone you to expect me." Manon Orliac ran her fingers through her hair and gazed off at the

Marne. "*Merde!*" She let her hand fall heavily against her thigh. "This is so t-t-typical of her."

"Of your mother?"

"She never does anything right."

"Wait," I said. "Your name is Manon Orliac, so your father. . . is. . . Tristan Orliac?"

"*Oui, bien sûr.*"

"And your mother is—?"

"Giselle Mounier."

If Mademoiselle Orliac had detonated a concussion grenade at that moment, I would have been less astonished. Giselle had never once, in the six years I had known her, even hinted that she had a daughter—she had always claimed to *dislike* children, in fact. And Giselle's lover (husband? ex-husband?) Tristan Orliac, whom I had also never heard of, turned out to be an international black marketeer bent on double-crossing the mother of his child, and maybe even his own child, in the bargain. Or maybe Tristan's daughter was in league with him against her mother!

"She t-t-told me I would be w-w-welcome to come by and see the painting, before you sold it tonight t-to the Count."

I thought I had volunteered for smuggling and fencing fine art purloined from Nazis, but it seemed instead that I was merely caught in a family feud, a family whose very existence Giselle had always kept hidden. When Giselle had said there were lots of things she had kept secret over the years, I'd never suspected the secret things were *human beings*.

"You're saying Giselle sent you, and not Tristan?"

"What d-d-difference does it make?"

Manon Orliac's stutter made her seem dangerous, because she punctuated every difficult consonant with an angry scowl, and her eyes became opaque and unreadable while she struggled with a word. Though she was small, even frail-looking,

I sensed a ruthlessness in her attitude that I had seen many times before in despairing revolutionaries. Her apparently unassuming posture actually marked the aplomb of a person with nothing to lose.

"Why do you want to see the painting?" I asked.

"Well, it's m-my money, isn't it?"

* * * * *

I excused myself and returned to the *Mirabelle*. Manon Orliac stood watching us from the street above as I explained the situation to Benoît. I then telephoned Giselle.

"I know I should have told you," Giselle said mawkishly, after many apologies and pleas for understanding. "But this whole episode has been so difficult for me, Luke, so sudden."

"Manon says the money from the painting belongs to her."

"I told her I'd give her part of my share."

"But what about the antique shop? What about all those debts?"

"This is one of them, Luke."

"Have you told me one straight thing yet?" I looked up the riverbank at Giselle's daughter. "Why did you send her here?"

"I didn't. She demanded to know what was happening, so I told her. I thought I owed her that much."

"You seem to owe her a lot!"

"I didn't think she'd go find you, Luke, honestly."

"That's not what she says."

"Well, Manon. . . she can't always be trusted." It was the purest instance I'd ever heard of the pot calling the kettle black.

"You think she's working for Tristan?"

"No, certainly not. She hates him even more than she hates

me. Oh, Luke, I'll explain it all when we're together again. It's complicated. Please trust me."

Giselle had now used my name four times in under a minute and asked me to trust her, which was laying it on a bit thick: her damsel-in-distress routine didn't have quite the power over the phone that it did in person. I disconnected the call and put the phone in my pocket.

"Well?" Benoît said.

"Beats the hell out of me."

The three of us stood looking from each other to Manon and back, Benoît and I especially astounded by this new development and what it meant to our ideas of Giselle. Apparently, sharing drinks with a woman at a bar is simply not a good way to get to know her.

The radio in the *Mirabelle*'s cabin crackled, and Regnault went to answer it. Benoît looked more and more exhausted, and he sat down again in a deck chair, put his elbows on his knees and propped his chin in the palms of his hands.

"We must not lose sight of the goal," Benoît said, "and it's not Giselle and her family problems. We're one meeting away from half a million euros."

Up on the banks, Manon Orliac threw up her hands. She came bounding down the steps to the promenade. She crossed the quay with an odd, staccato gait, more like stomping than walking, and marched up to the *Mirabelle*'s gangplank. "Look," she said. "I just want to see it. I l-l-love Maximilien Luce, and I have a *right* to see it."

This utterly unmotivated admission, that Manon loved Maximilien Luce, convinced me all at once of her honesty. It was such an unnecessary declaration, especially in combination with her petulant assertion of a non-existent right to see the painting, that I could not help trusting her sincerity, and I thought her boldness so quintessentially French that I was charmed by the useless beauty of it. She was vehement and grim, claiming theoretical privileges whose enforcement made no real sense and whose only immediate profit was aesthetic. Beyond that, her monetary interest in ransoming the painting rested on the trampling of someone else's rights in favor of her own, and it directly contradicted her own professed love of the artist, since she could only realize her share in the money by depriving herself and the general public of Luce's work. Such a wealth of paradoxes in so terse a statement epitomized the reasons I loved and hated the French, and it suddenly decided me on a new course of action.

"You can see the painting," I said, "but only if you help me take it to the Luxembourg Gardens."

"*Quoi*?" Benoît exclaimed. "*Il n'en est pas question!* Absolutely not!"

"I don't think we can just sit here with those goons tied up in the cabin and Dumesnil still on the loose," I said. "We've broadcast our presence here, and we're just asking for someone to come along and take that painting."

"Yeah, and that someone is named Orliac, and here she is! Besides, last night you said there was strength in numbers."

Regnault returned from the captain's cabin. He looked up and down the quay and then across the river to the lock-keeper's station.

"I'm not saying it makes sense," I said, "but I believe her." I looked into Manon's ruthless, gray-spangled eyes and felt comfortable with her, in a way that my gut could not fully explain to my mind. "Anyway, the hairs on my arms are standing up—something bad is about to happen here, and she's not it."

Benoît shook his head no. "You've lost your mind!"

"Think of it this way—every successful operation depends on a little luck, and Manon might be our little luck."

"No," Benoît said, "it's a trick."

"It kills me to agree with him, Benoît," Regnault interrupted. "But I think your friend here might be right." He then told us that he had just been speaking to the lock-keeper, who had alerted him that there was suddenly a lot of radio chatter about the *Mirabelle*.

"What does that mean?" I asked.

Regnault spat into the Marne. "I'm trying to take your side, you imbecile! If you're keeping a secret and all at once everyone's talking about you, then perhaps your secret isn't such a secret any more."

"But if you take the painting in Giselle's convertible," Benoît said, "they'll recognize it. They'll follow you."

"They're more likely to follow the *Mirabelle*," Regnault countered. "That's where the trail leads. Up to this minute, both the painting and Orliac's men have stopped here, and people are talking about my boat, not about her car. No one even knows she's involved, right?" Regnault nodded toward Manon.

"I'm n-n-not involved," Manon asserted, contrary to all available evidence.

"See?" Regnault continued. "We've got to clean this situation up—ditch the painting, ditch these thugs and head upriver. We'll lead them on a wild goose chase, and by the time they realize we don't have the painting on board, your friends will already have the money. Right? Let's think how we can best get *the money*!"

This turn of events, so typical in moments of crisis and yet so unpredictable, made me feel exhilarated just to be alive. I felt that in a moment of providence we had gained an unlooked-for ally in Manon, and the operation was now taking a more organic if improvised shape: Regnault would serve as a decoy, Manon would serve as a courier, and after much confusion it seemed we were now half a step ahead of our enemies, instead of struggling to catch up.

In that moment, I believed that we had turned a critical corner, that my intuition about the presence of imminent danger had been justified, and that my luck was finally guiding us all in the right direction.

* * * * *

With *La Seine à Herblay* in the back seat, still rolled up in its black waterproof tube, Manon and I raced away from the quay in Alfort and back toward Paris. I phoned Giselle to inform her of the new developments, and she said she'd meet us at the main fountain right below the Luxembourg Palace.

As a driver, Manon was *une moyenne parisienne*: she lead-footed it around slower traffic, blew through the beginnings of red lights and squealed around corners. "N-not many kids get a sports car for their f-first vehicle, eh?" she said. At Pont d'Austerlitz, she merged toward the bridge, then power-shifted into an exit lane, cutting off a taxi; then just as suddenly she swerved back onto the bridge in front of a hulking delivery truck, at the very last possible second before plunging into the Seine. We screeched to a halt just centimeters from the car in front of us as traffic stopped

"Giselle gave you her car?" I said, trying to sound calm.

As we hurtled toward the Luxembourg Gardens, Manon gave me a curt summary of her relationship with Giselle and Tristan Orliac and her involvement in the affair of the Luce painting. She told the story disinterestedly, concentrating more on the road in front of her, as if her whole life had happened to someone else.

Manon was the result of a youthful indiscretion between Giselle and Tristan, which their well-to-do families were ashamed of and which Giselle and Tristan themselves apparently regretted. Manon had been shuttled between the Orliac and Mounier families for most of her life, raised by aunts and grandparents, and her relationship with her parents resembled the relationship of a cousin to much older, distant cousins. The fact that Tristan and Giselle hated one another had only exacerbated Manon's situation, and she had been on civil terms with her parents only since she had started university the previous autumn and moved into her own apartment.

Giselle had called Manon out of the blue two days before to promise her a large sum of money, and though the sudden gift was not explained, Manon had seen the money as reparations for years of neglect. However, Giselle had shown up at Manon's apartment not with money or even explanations, but with torn clothing and terror in her eyes. Giselle gave Manon the keys to her BMW, told her the car was hers now, and then fled. Only minutes later, as Manon stood on the sidewalk confoundedly examining her new car, her father's goons arrived and, unaware of Manon's identity, roughed her up a bit in search of the Luce. Manon called her father and viciously attacked him for this abuse, and Tristan had reluctantly confessed the whole sordid situation.

Manon, recognizing the opportunity before her, had then gone to her mother's antique shop, stolen Giselle's laptop and some of her files, and was determined to sort the whole mess out by herself, to her own profit. She thought the fact that she was intimately familiar with Maximilien Luce and the Pointillists through her university studies might help her in some way, but she was incapable of turning her abstract love of art into a concrete plan for fencing a painting, especially since she didn't actually have the painting. Instead, she settled on phoning her father incessantly, haranguing him and slyly giving him false clues about the whereabouts of Giselle and the Luce, to keep him away from her mother while she tried to make the sale.

Despite Manon's stutter, her thoughts were remarkably fluid and she told her tale with biting wit. Her whole demeanor—from her candidness to her simple outmoded clothing, unkempt hair and wild hand gestures—suggested the diametrical opposite of her mother. That is, the opposite of the rigid persona that her mother showed to the world.

"And now your mother has obviously told you about the rendezvous tonight with Count Dumesnil?"

"I can usually w-wear her down with guilt, until she confesses. My m-mother is not the m-most responsible person in the world, but she can be shrewd and even. . . c-c-cunning in a pinch. I believe she can p-pull this off, and I would frankly l-like my life to be a little easier—so in this one instance, I'm r-r-rooting for her, and I w-want the money."

As we entered the Saint-Germain-des-Pres district, Manon stared intently into the rearview mirror. "Someone's f-following us," she said. I turned and looked. "A blue Saab." I picked out the Saab, several car lengths back in a different lane.

"You sure?"

"He's been back there since r-rue de Paris."

For someone to have kept pace with Manon's maniacal driving from rue de Paris to boulevard Diderot and then across the bridge to the Left Bank would have been quite a feat. "Do you think you can lose him?"

"I d-don't know," she smiled. "I've been trying."

We drove rapidly along the Left Bank, until we made a sudden left onto a side street. Manon accelerated through a changing light and then whipped across traffic onto boulevard Saint-Germain. We dodged in and out of traffic until we came to another little side street, which bent away at a thirty-five degree angle. We followed it for several blocks and then took a sharp right at rue Racine—almost a U-turn, because Racine doubles back toward the river at a hundred-fifteen degree angle. We then skidded around a corner onto rue Monsieur Le Prince, which curves along an obtuse arc toward the Seine. Essentially, we had made three right turns and driven in a complicated rhombus back to where we had started on boulevard Saint-Germain.

"Look," she pointed straight ahead of us.

I stared for a few seconds before I found the Saab again, now about five car lengths ahead of us. We had circled around it, and now *we* were chasing *him*. "Some p-people don't really know how to drive." Manon snailed ahead, deliberately putting more and more distance between us and our pursuer, until a red light separated us completely from the Saab. As the blue car disappeared into the traffic ahead, Manon turned off toward the Luxembourg Gardens.

* * * * *

The Luxembourg *quartier* is one of the wealthiest in Paris, with palatial apartments, Michelin three-star restaurants and many practically intact remnants of the *Ancien Regime*. The centerpiece of the quarter is the Palace itself, an Italian-style chateau that Marie de Medicis built to console herself on the assassination of her husband, King Henri IV, in 1610. The Palace now houses the French senate, but it has also been a prison (during the French Revolution) and headquarters for the German Luftwaffe (during the Second World War), a fact whose connection to my present mission did not escape me.

Attached to the Palace is a sixty-acre garden, the most popular outdoor spot in Paris, and therefore a good place to lose yourself in a crowd. Moreover, Giselle had told me that the Dumesnil family owned property in this area, and I intended to suggest that we meet the Count right here for the ransom exchange.

Manon parked the Z8 near a cafe in front of the garden's north gate. I stood watch while she wedged herself behind the driver's seat and unfurled the Luce. How she could even unroll the painting all the way in that cramped passenger compartment, much less make out the beautiful pixilations, was beyond me, but when she emerged after a few moments with the black tube, she seemed satisfied. She showed me a corner of the canvas before she sealed the tube, in a scrupulous display of trustworthiness, and then she handed it over to me.

We walked into the gardens. We were hardly inconspicuous even among the bustling crowds: I was limping and haggard and leaned on Manon for support, my arm around her tiny shoulders. Regnault's black tube, perfectly invisible when floating illicit cargo underneath a *péniche*, was a beacon of strangeness in the afternoon sunshine.

We proceeded as casually as possible through a long arbor of chestnut and plane trees, observing the little grottoes with reflecting pools and the grandiose fountains with absurdly rococo bronze statuary. There were sandboxes for children, tennis courts and outdoor displays of arts and crafts for adults. Every corner was alive with activity. An accordian-playing Moroccan was singing for spare change on the landscaped promenade; a teenager danced with her pet rabbit, which chewed at the hem of her sleeve; an old man stood on a bench, manipulating a nearly life-sized marionette of the French president. Two old women strolling near us were arguing fiercely about some intricacy in the rules of bridge.

"There's my m-mother," Manon said, as we emerged from beneath the trees and approached the regimented shrubberies below the Palace. The enormous open square, with its severely mown greenswards and gravel paths leading to the fountain, was so overrun by shouting children and their admonishing parents that it took me a moment to find Giselle. She was sitting on a green wooden bench, still wearing my t-shirt and blue jeans. On the ground beside her, leaning against the bench, was an artist's portfolio.

"I'm g-going to leave you now."

"You don't want to see your mother? Or come with us?" I liked Manon and thought she might prove a valuable asset.

"I think your f-friend the b-barge captain had the right idea. I'm going to drive around a little and maybe serve as a d-decoy." She let go of my waist and turned to look me in the eye. "I know you don't know me, Luke, but I'm c-c-counting on you. I've heard a lot about you over the years, and I h-hope I can trust you."

She kissed me on both cheeks and then stomped with her martial steps back the way we came. I watched her until she melted into the teeming arms and legs and shirts of other people.

Giselle was intently watching children race hand-made wooden sailboats across the pool when I touched her gently on the shoulder. She jumped, and then grabbed onto my forearm in relief. Though my mind had been filled with complaints and accusations to direct at her, all my rancor evaporated when she touched me, and I found her even more attractive than I had the day before, when we'd made love. I reminded myself that she had done little but hurt me in the last two days, and I found the revelations about her neglect of her daughter distasteful, but this did not make her less attractive to me. On the contrary, despite the real danger she had put me in, and despite the emotional darkness of her double life, I found her more sympathetic and alluring than ever. But then, I still like Barbara Stanwyk better than Fred MacMurray in *Double Indemnity*, even knowing how it all comes out.

Giselle scooted over to make room for me on the bench. "Ah, *mon mignon*," she said, combing my hair back from my forehead, "what on earth happened to you?"

Because my knee had been giving me the most trouble since my encounter with the two thugs, I forgot that my face had also been tenderized like a veal scallopini. "The black market happened to me," I said quietly. "You pick some fine playmates."

She petted my head and face. "Well, we don't have to play with them any more—I'm through with the black market. I realize now that I'm too naive to deal with those guys."

"Right," I said, "from now on we'll deal exclusively with Nazis. That should simplify matters."

She sat very close to me, her leg touching mine. The delicacy with which she stroked my cheek reminded me of Séverine's caresses at my apartment the morning before, after she had found me beaten up by those same two thugs.

"If you hated Tristan so much and you knew you couldn't trust him, why did you try to make this deal through him in the first place?"

Giselle shrugged. "I knew he had connections, and I needed it done fast."

"And why didn't you ever tell anyone about Manon?"

She looked away and affected a world-weary tone. "It's complicated, you know."

Complicated: this was so typical of the French, who will shout the most shocking and outrageous political critiques or religious opinions in every public square but are scandalized by even commonplace family difficulties, which they would rather carry to their graves than reveal to their closest friends. I found it especially irritating that Giselle hadn't even asked about her daughter when I'd arrived alone, even though she knew we had come to the gardens together.

"Anyway, it doesn't matter now," she said. "This whole business will be over soon enough, and then we can go away together and forget about all this."

"About that little detail," I said. "I'm really in no position to go away with you. I mean, there's Séverine, my work. . ." I let my voice trail off because, looking into Giselle's eyes, I found that I actually wanted to go away with her. Maybe the French were right: maybe it was complicated!

"Those aren't exactly resounding rejections, Luke. You never work in Paris, so you could easily make your headquarters anywhere in the world and still fly off to wherever your assignments take you. And you forget that I know your history with Séverine."

"Maybe, but it's looking a lot more solid than my history with you, which started just two days ago. I'm not even sure who you are any more, and I'm not convinced that you know, either." I looked at some of the young boys launching sailboats in the octagonal pool a few meters away. "Anyway, I'm absolutely not going to the Opéra-Comique tonight, and I resent your trying to force my hand that way. Séverine is going to throw a fit in any event when she finds out that I went ahead with this scheme, but if we make the drop there, she'll never speak to me again."

"She doesn't have to know about it. Won't she be backstage working?"

"Then why do it there? You see? Just admit that that's what you wanted, that you're trying to force my hand and show up Séverine, and then we can forget about it and find a new location. Like how about the grotto just around the corner?"

The Fountaine de Medicis was nearby, a burbling fountain below a Baroque sculpture of Roman gods. It's an area quiet enough to facilitate an illegal exchange but still public enough to discourage grandstanding double-crosses.

"Doesn't the Count live in this area, anyway?" I said. "These gardens would be the most logical meeting place for all of us."

"He does have a home near here, but he's in Reims right now. He'll be coming in this evening to the Opéra-Comique."

"There's no reason he couldn't come here instead."

"You know, Luke, we should really get you cleaned up. Doesn't your cheek hurt?"

I admitted that my whole body felt like scrap iron. "But don't change the subject."

"Everything's already arranged," Giselle said, "and it was no mean feat getting the Count to agree to the exchange the way it is. I don't want to foul it all up now."

"That's awfully feeble."

"Why don't we go back to my apartment and talk about this? I'll put some ice on that bruise."

"We can't go anywhere anyone might expect us to be." I told her about the Saab that had chased Manon and me through Saint-Germain-des-Pres and the lock-keeper's warning that someone was hunting the *Mirabelle*. "Somebody's obviously onto us, and I doubt that it's just the Count."

"How about a hotel? The Montalembert and the Relais Manon are both near here."

I nearly choked. "Those are two of the most expensive hotels in Paris. You wouldn't prefer an *auberge*? Or a cardboard box beneath a bridge?"

"It's not like we can't afford it," Giselle said.

"*You* certainly can't. Remember, we don't actually have any money yet, just a canvas with a bunch of bright dots on it."

Giselle sighed. "Why can't you see this as an incredible opportunity? Why do you have to be so negative all the time?"

"I'm negative all the time?"

"Yes. You never see possibilities, you only ever see obstacles."

I'm sure my expression became comical—we were having

a lovers' quarrel! "Maybe I'm so negative because people keep beating me unconscious. But I'm trying to see the silver lining, *cherie*, I'm trying."

Giselle folded her arms across her chest. I rolled my eyes. Any more of this and we'd need couples counseling.

"Come on," she said. She stood up. "If you're not going to take care of yourself, I guess I'll have to take care of you." This statement was so rich with irony that my mind went completely blank. "Come on," she insisted. She held her hand out to me, palm upward, and wiggled her fingers for me to stand up. I stood up. She rubbed my back and leaned her body into mine, and I recognized, with an electric surprise at the absurdity of this joke, that I had fallen hopelessly in love with Giselle.

13

A Question of Values

Giselle escorted me to a taxi stand just outside the Luxembourg Gardens. She told our driver to take us to the Hôtel des Deux-Îles—not exactly a budget inn—on Île Saint Louis. Beyond its fancy price tag, it was right around the corner from Séverine's apartment, and I marveled at Giselle's faultless psychological marksmanship: we had to pass by Séverine's place to get to the hotel, so it was impossible for me to escape the implications of what I was doing. At every turn, she was flaunting the fact that I was cheating on Séverine by being with her. Why this invidious boldness attracted me to her, I'm not entirely sure, but it did.

On the ride over, I paid special attention to the cars trailing us and the pedestrians along the avenues, but no one jumped out at me as an obvious threat. There was no blue Saab, no black Mercedes, and the people along the route to the hotel seemed ordinarily forgettable, rather than intentionally nondescript the way a spy might be. I believed that our multiple decoys had baffled our pursuers—such is the arrogance of amateurs.

When we entered the ostentatiously luxurious lobby of the Hôtel des Deux-Îles, the desk clerk eyed me with clear disdain. I glimpsed myself in the gold-framed mirror above the reception desk: between the olive-colored contusion on my cheek and the dishevelment of my rather déclassé sports coat, I looked unfit to clean the hotel's grease trap, and everyone cast worried glances at my black tube, as if it might be a homemade bomb. The clerk didn't seem convinced by Giselle either—her t-shirt and artist's portfolio failed to make her look artistic, and artists couldn't afford this hotel, anyway.

When Giselle asked if she could charge the room to her shop, the clerk looked even more dubious and called the manager. However, it turned out that Giselle knew the manager personally, and her recommendations had brought the hotel quite a lot of business in the past. Giselle and the manager had a polite conversation (how's the shop? hot weather we've been having!), and despite the questionable nature of our errand there and my ratty appearance, he granted Giselle's request. A suite was billed to Giselle's shop, and a bellhop escorted us to the fourth floor.

Giselle had so much good will in so many places, I thought— how could she have lived a double life for so long? How could she have descended to the brink of financial ruin, to crimes of larceny and violence? She was an object lesson in the value of living an authentic life—a life as true in appearance as it is in fact—and if I hadn't been embezzling art and cheating on my girlfriend at that moment, I might have appreciated the lesson even more.

The suite was air-conditioned, as almost no buildings in downtown Paris are, and I was grateful for the cool, dry air. I flung the black tube into a chair and fell back onto the queen-size bed. The downy softness of the bed's coverlet felt good along my entire body, and I breathed deeply and closed my eyes, unaware until that moment how much I needed rest.

I felt Giselle's weight on the mattress. She had slipped out of my blue jeans, and now she stood on her knees over me, wearing only my t-shirt and boxer shorts and a mischievous grin.

"I'm tired, Giselle. I thought you were going to take care of me."

"I *am* going to take care of you."

She removed the t-shirt and then curled up next to my head, kissing my bruised cheek and breathing wetly into my ear. She rubbed her breasts all over my face, down to my neck, while gently pulling my shirt out of my pants. Then she did something I never expected in a million years: she spit on my cheek and massaged her own saliva into my bruise with her tongue. Though I doubted the medicinal value of rubbing spit into a contusion, the act was eerily erotic.

She licked my entire face, like a cat, and then she opened my mouth with her fingers and spit a big glob of saliva into it. I was so surprised that I gasped, and some of her spit entered my windpipe. I choked and coughed. She waited until the fit passed, then she kissed me on the mouth with her own mouth open, swishing her tongue around the inside of my lips. This woman was stranger than I had ever imagined, but I had to admit that I had stopped thinking about my injuries.

Giselle took my pants off and repeated this spitting and licking on my wounded knee. Then she slid my underwear off and repeated it again, in a way that did not seem quite so strange and that made me forget not only my injuries but my whole self. For this momentary obliteration—a loss of consciousness as complicated and vulgar as any of the others I'd experienced recently, but indisputably sweeter—I felt grateful.

* * * * *

I napped in Giselle's arms, until she roused me from sleep and took me into the bathroom. She drew a warm bath for me, just as I had done for her earlier, at Séverine's apartment. While the tub was filling, she went into the hotel corridor to fetch some ice.

She bathed me and applied ice, off and on, to my neck and face and knee, alternating hot and cold, until my swelling began to come down and the pain genuinely receded. She ladled warm water over my body with her hands and caressed me from head to foot. When the bath water turned cool, I stood up and she dried me with a plush white hotel towel.

She finally took off the boxers she was wearing, so that we were both completely naked, and we stood in the bathroom looking into one another's eyes. Her eyes seemed to get larger the longer I looked into them—I felt like I was being hypnotized, but by the time I had consciously had that thought, it was far too late to escape. We returned to bed and lay in each other's arms.

* * * * *

"I'm still not going to the Opéra-Comique tonight," I said later, as we snuggled under the covers. We had turned the air conditioning on high, and the room was now frigid. We burrowed deep into the heavy hotel blankets. "You have to call the Count. Tell him to meet us at Luxembourg Gardens."

"All right," Giselle said. "Hand me Jean-Pierre's mobile phone."

I got the phone from the front pocket of her blue jeans and handed it to her. She dialed a number from memory, had a brief conversation with someone on the other end of the line, then announced that Dumesnil was no longer in Reims. She dialed another number, had another brief conversation, then hung up and announced that the Count wasn't in Paris yet, either.

"Call him on his cell phone," I said.

"He doesn't have one."

"Doesn't have one? Surely he has businesses to deal with

or stock portfolios to manage? I thought everybody but the barge people had cell phones these days."

"He's not in touch the way normal people are. He has plenty of business interests to manage, but he pays other people to keep track of it all."

"Yeah, they can keep track of everything but his stolen art collection."

"That *is* funny, isn't it?" said Giselle. She yawned and kissed my neck. "If I were a psychologist, I'd say he *wanted* to show me that art collection—he wanted to get caught. The only reason he was having his stuff appraised in the first place was his mother's death, so maybe there was some Oedipal thing going on with his mother. Now that she's dead, he just wants out of the whole affair, he wants to get away from everything that reminds him of her, and he's begging for someone to bring the whole dirty secret into the light."

"You don't know anything about psychology, do you?"

"Do you?"

"No."

She kissed my lips and we were silent for a long while. Finally, as if musing aloud to herself, Giselle said, "He thinks life worked much better in the fourteenth century. He spends as much time as he can at his castle, just being a Count, and modern-day things like cell phones or satellite television or democracy don't make sense to him. He uses an actual human courier to deliver his messages—he doesn't like voice mail or e-mail or even mail mail. He never even answers his phone— people answer for him and then other people are dispatched to tell him he has a phone call, and he usually just gives them a message to give the caller. At least, that's how it worked with me, till I stole his painting.

"When I first met him, I thought he was really out of touch, but the fact is just the contrary: he usually knows exactly what's going on, where everything and everyone is at every moment, without a two-way pager or surveillance cameras or fancy alarm systems. He keeps it all in his head. That's why I imagine he's so angry about this mess. It was just sheer negligence on his own part—a momentary lapse of vigilance—and he has no one but himself to blame."

"He could blame you."

"But I would never have known about the painting if he hadn't left me alone that first day of my appraisal, if he hadn't left the door to his secret vault open. Why did he do that?"

"I guess it *is* cleaner to blame him, isn't it?" I said. "Why don't you call the Count's hired men back and tell them the location for the rendezvous has been changed? Maybe they'll dispatch a homing pigeon to give him the message."

Giselle phoned the Count's Paris apartments and left Jean-Pierre's mobile number with his servants. She then dropped the phone to the floor—it was clear that she had her heart set on going to the Opéra-Comique. She was intent on asserting her claim to me in front of Séverine.

* * * * *

The Hôtel des Deux-Îles was certainly not the worst place you could find to hole up and wait, so I stopped fretting and ordered room service. We had never expected to come here, so it was difficult to imagine anyone else expecting us here either. I called the Happy Elephant while we waited for our food to arrive.

"I was beginning to worry," said Jean-Pierre. In fact, his voice was especially gravely with cigarette smoke, and I knew he had been worried all day.

"I'm sorry," I said. "But I have good news. I won't burden you with the details, but everybody's fine and we should be rid of the thing tonight, at a tidy profit. We're thinking of celebrating at the Elephant tonight."

"Never plan a celebration till you actually have something to celebrate," he said.

"You know, sometimes you sound just like me."

"But most of the time *you* sound just like *me*." He paused to inhale a Gitane. "Anyway, I'm glad you're all right," he said, and then he abruptly hung up, almost before he had finished the sentence. It was his way of saying I was an asshole for mistreating Séverine.

* * * * *

We ate in bed—filleted duck's breast, cooked extremely rare, and fried potatoes and fennel, followed by my favorite ice cream, pear-and-candied-chestnut sherbet—and my opinion of the hotel rose steadily. This kind of luxury, after all, was why people coveted money in the first place, and I was not immune to its charms.

Giselle took a long bath, and I spread the painting out on the dresser in the corner. Would you want half a million euros, I said to myself, or this picture of the Seine? How could anyone in his right mind prefer this painting over *half a million* euros? In order to place such outrageous value on individual objects, no matter how rare, the Count must have had tens of millions and more, and thinking about such sums staggered my imagination; but then, I thought, how was that so different from what Giselle and I were doing in this damned expensive hotel? Wouldn't I want to be like the Count, to have so much wealth that half a million euros looked like decorating money? Already, just by living month to month in a tiny hole-in-the-wall apartment in the Marais, I had vastly more money than the people I sold photographs of—desperately poor people in Rwanda or Haiti or Kashmir—and I began to appreciate Giselle's conflicted attitude toward value more deeply.

The Count placed value on objects in a way that only people with vast sums of discretionary income could do, and there was something queasy about the fact that the Count would give enough money to support a Cambodian village for a generation just for this one picture. A Louis XV armoire and a bargain-basement pressboard cabinet were equally valuable to a poor person, after all, since aesthetics add monetary value only when a thing's function no longer determines its worth. When the aesthetic value of a useful object becomes primary, the concept of value itself can easily turn into a hall of mirrors, and somehow this extremely abstract concept gave me a pang of love for Giselle.

It *was* a beautiful painting, I thought. I propped the canvas against the wall and backed across the room to appreciate its full effect. I found it more beautiful the more I looked at it, and in only two days I had even grown somewhat attached to it.

To the extent that I knew the difference between a good photograph and a poor one, I understood how someone might value a great photograph more than money—the more sophisticated side of me understood how monetary value could be placed on beauty, how someone could pay a fortune for a singular painting that touched his soul. But this painting represented more of a fortune than I could ever aspire to, and yet it represented merely an inconvenient expenditure to the Count, and it was this difference in scale that made my mind reel.

Giselle, I thought, had been living in a secret hell of wildly inflated values, while her own moral failings with her daughter must have weighed heavily on her as well. I unexpectedly felt a wave of admiration for Séverine as I reflected on it. Séverine had not been infected with the same ambivalence, and the abstract calculations of value in the fashion world remained completely transparent to her. Séverine had always been a pragmatist who designed outlandish fashions for dreamers, and she held the contradictions of her position in her head with no effort at all. Her pragmatism suddenly seemed much more sophisticated than I had previously imagined, and Séverine had never abandoned her own child to her relatives.

I wished I could love both Giselle and Séverine at the same time. But then, that was a different kind of value altogether.

* * * * *

Giselle continued to call the Count's Paris home throughout the afternoon and into the evening without reaching the Count himself, and I grew more and more uneasy. As the evening wore on and we received no word, I became worried about the simple fact of his absence: whether we made the exchange at the Opéra-Comique or Luxembourg Gardens or anywhere else, we still needed someone to make the exchange with, and I was wary of another double-cross.

It didn't take long to drive from Reims to Paris on the autoroute, so where could Dumesnil be? Getting the cash? Maybe, but I wondered about the connection between the blue Saab and the Count, or the blue Saab and the painting without the Count. Contrary to Benoît's assertion that this was a done deal, I felt that there were many unexplained things still happening and many potentially dangerous loose ends that we couldn't quite tie together.

I ordered a bottle of aspirin from room service, and as I chased down a handful with a glass of mineral water, I had an epiphany: I suddenly realized why I loved going to war, and why I had been so attracted to this cockamamie art heist in the first place. Séverine had been wrong—it wasn't that I loved courting death. What I loved was the anticipation of action, the prospect that something life-altering was about to happen, any moment now, a prospect that was sorely missing in the humdrum world of eight-to-five jobs. It didn't matter how brutal or revolting the action might be, and it didn't even matter that my own life might be altered beyond recognition, or that I might be killed. I wanted to live in a world of novel possibilities, and this combination—the anticipation of sudden change and then the change itself, in whatever form it took—was like a drug rush. It wasn't the difference between life and death that fascinated me, it was the difference between life and an entirely different kind of life, and in that Giselle and I were alike. The frustration of waiting and worrying was also the delicious prospect of change.

Once I understood that simple fact, I actually stopped worrying altogether. I sat back in bed and punched up a pay movie on the house cable system—an action movie—and I enjoyed the certainty that, one way or another, something exciting and life-changing was about to happen.

14

Haute Couture

By seven o'clock in the evening, we still had not reached the Count, and it became clear that if we were going to make the drop that night then we would have to do so at the Opéra-Comique.

It was still possible, I thought, to pull this exchange off and keep Séverine temporarily in the dark. Giselle's fatuous and confrontational assertion that Séverine would be backstage during the actual show was correct, after all, so that if the swap went off without a hitch, out in the gallery, the fashionistas in their dressing rooms would be none the wiser. Séverine would eventually learn that I was there, of course—I had no press or industry credentials, so I would have to use the personal contacts I had made through Séverine in order to enter the show, and those people would no doubt mention that I was in the theater. But I imagined I could use even this to my advantage: once we had settled the business with the Count, I could duck backstage and say hello, playing the dutiful boyfriend arriving to give support and encouragement.

Looking back on it now, I see that these were lunatic notions, and my gut was telling me to pull the rip cord and jump out of the whole scheme. My heart, though, loves the risk of love as much as it loves love, and I realize in hindsight that my head's hedging—my need to keep possibilities open with both Séverine and Giselle—was the main reason that the affair with the painting ended the way it did. My gut and my heart were at odds, and in those cases, my head always winds up being the final arbiter. My head, it turns out, is the real problem.

* * * * *

Fashion shows typically take place late in the evening, and Paris fashion shows run later than any in the world. No one in couture circles even finishes dinner before ten o'clock, and designers prefer that their audiences be as fully sated as possible before the spectacle begins, so that the mellow mood of self-satisfaction can translate into positive press and lucrative sales. To this end, there are usually champagne receptions before the shows, and in places like the Crazy Horse Cabaret or the Lido—dinner-theater venues—there may be a five-course pre-show meal for the VIPs. The last thing designers want after their shows is to have sober reporters calmly deliberating their designs, so runway models never take the stage until the fashion scribes have had a full evening of wine and flattery.

Giselle had therefore arranged to meet the Count at the Opéra-Comique at eleven, when the first blush of excitement would still be filling the hall, and the audience would be suitably distracted by the pomp and spectacle. Giselle had transferred the Luce from the black tube to her artist's portfolio. The portfolio would not be out of place at a fashion show, and Giselle had arranged a simple swap with the Count: the portfolio for a briefcase full of money. It was somewhat less than Hitchcockian in its cleverness, but it would at least arouse no suspicions. Next, we needed to change into suitable evening attire for the show, so we had the hotel call us a taxi at nine o'clock, and we headed for my apartment.

It was still fully light when we piled into the cab: the summer sun was just beginning to approach the horizon, and as we rolled slowly down the narrow one-way street that fronts the hotel, I searched for the Count or Tristan Orliac's henchmen or anyone else I recognized who might have designs on the Luce, but we seemed clear and free for the moment. I actually did see the buttery blonde man who was following us—in the driver's seat of a brown Renault Clio right behind our taxi—but I would realize that he was following us only in retrospect, after he had surprised us at the Opera.

We had the taxi wait on the street below my apartment. I changed into a Corneliani shirt (*très chic*), with Hugo Boss slacks (*à la page*) and a Canali sport coat (all courtesy of Séverine). Then we went to Giselle's apartment north of Les Halles. We asked the taxi driver to go up first to reconnoiter (he complied for an extra twenty), and when he said everything seemed in order, we paid him and sent him on his way, in order to avoid leaving a trail directly from the hotel to the Opera. Giselle changed into a classic black Chanel pantsuit—not cutting edge fashion, but perennially stylish, and she would at least not stick out.

We still had a little while before dark, before it was time to head for the rendezvous, and I spent the time pacing, staring furtively out the window looking for threats. I tried to imagine the extremely old-fashioned Count at such an avant-garde fashion event. He would have no trouble getting through the doors: the Dumesnil name was sufficiently well-known to *le tout Paris* that he would be recognized and catered to. The only thing fashion people respect more than money is celebrity, and the Count had just enough of both to cause a stir, so the first order of business would be to get him alone. This might not be easy in a place where his mere presence would be a curiosity.

I pictured the exchange over and over again, in different sections of the Opera, using creative visualization the way a champion athlete might. Setting the portfolio down on the ground next to the Count's briefcase, making a polite remark, stretching my arms, then bending down and picking up the money. Who would even care?

I was still concerned that the Count might pull a switch or give us an empty briefcase, but Giselle assured me of his sincerity. "If he stiffs us," she said, "we'll just blow the whistle on him, and he'll lose everything."

"Then why wouldn't he just kill us and eliminate that danger once and for all? How can he live with the constant risk of exposure hanging over his head?"

"You don't really understand blackmail, do you?"

"No, and you don't understand power."

"If he kills us, how is he going to get the painting back?"

"He can kill us *after* we make the swap," I said. "Tomorrow, for instance."

I didn't understand why Benoît and Giselle weren't worried for their lives after the deal went down. In the Colombian cocaine trade, if someone stole something of value from you and then tried to ransom it back, you'd kill the thief and the thief's whole family, and then you might kill the thief's neighbors' pets just as a warning. I had seen dogs hanging from trees in Medellin more than once, and though the Count was no drug lord, he *was* a Nazi collaborator. Or at least his mother had been. Anyway, he had already shot at me.

"He won't have to kill us," Giselle said, "because there's no chance we'll blow his cover after he pays us off. If we go to the police with the information, he'll reveal our ransom swindle and we'll all end up in jail. It's simple, Luke."

"Why won't he kill us just for revenge? He won't have to, but he might just want to."

"Revenge?" Giselle said. "This isn't some tribal squabble in the African bush. We're talking about someone with something to lose."

I was flabbergasted. It was the exact same opinion that Benoît had—that this was just crime, not war—and I wondered if I was completely out of touch with the "civilized" world or if my friends had simply never seen power exercised in a real way. As I sat there in my designer leisure wear, I began to think that the only place I really belonged was crouched in a jungle hut, hiding from mortar fire. That, at least, I understood.

* * * * *

The Opéra-Comique is within easy walking distance of Giselle's apartment, but we were so close to getting the money that I wanted to take no chances parading the painting around on the street: at ten-fifteen we called another cab. The buttery blonde man who had followed us from the hotel was waiting for us on the street—he had switched from his brown Renault Clio to a yellow Fiat Spider. I can see it so clearly in my memory, but I paid no attention to it at the time. My gut, usually so reliable, had abandoned me once I'd decided to follow my head to the Opera, so no alarm bells sounded at all.

We had the cabbie let us out on the corner half a block from our destination. The main entrance to the Opéra-Comique is at Place Boieldieu, but my intention was to use the side entrance, to maintain as low a profile as possible.

As its name suggests, the Opéra-Comique is dedicated to light musical theater, zany operettas and Broadway-style farce. The architect who built the theater, however, did not necessarily have this purpose in mind: the building is grand in design and extravagant in detail, with ornately carved cornices, high pediment windows and stone garlands festooning fluted gables. The outside of the theater has three levels: the first two stories are supported by simple Corinthian columns, but the uppermost tier features columns carved in the shapes of robed women. The women appear to be holding the roof on their shoulders, in poses suggesting that the weight of the pediments gives them a sensual pleasure.

Where normally the masks of comedy and tragedy might hang around a theater, the Opéra-Comique displays only the mask of comedy: laughing stone faces appear every ten meters along the dentils just below the roof, around the entire building. First seeing this theater is like first seeing a circus clown when you're a child—it seems both ominous and laughable, and you're not sure who the joke is going to be on.

We walked along the outside of the Opera. There weren't many people milling around, which I took as a good sign: the guests were already inside and the designers and models were already backstage cranking themselves tight for the show.

The fifteen-foot tall wooden doors along the side were locked, but I pounded on them and waited. When nothing happened, I knocked continuously until I heard scuffling from inside, and then someone shouted that we should use the front entrance. I pounded some more, until the voice inside told me to fuck off. We went around to the front.

At Place Boieldieu—a cobblestoned pedestrian square with two lighted fountains—thirty or forty people were standing in groups, smoking and talking. I recognized a journalist from *Mode* magazine and waved hello, and he shouted, "Evening, Luke. Where's your *hat*?" By his tone and gesture, I interpreted his remark as snide commentary on the fact that I was there with someone other than Séverine—everybody in the fashion world, no matter what gender, profession or rank, is catty. "You mind your wardrobe and I'll mind mine," I said. He raised his eyebrows at me and laughed nastily.

We walked up the Opera's wide concrete steps, past the stately Greek columns, to the main entrance, where blue-coated ushers were checking credentials. I greeted the ushers as if we utterly and unquestionably belonged there, but this ploy didn't impress them and we were stopped at the door.

As I began to explain who I was and who Séverine was, I caught the eye of Noëlle Prébois, the Opéra-Comique's publicity director, who was sashaying through the lobby with a champagne flute in each hand. She shouted a hearty, half-drunken greeting, nodded "okay" to the ushers and waved us into the lobby. We stepped through the metal detectors and walked inside, and the atmosphere instantly changed from run-of-the-mill Paris to high pretension Empire: we were in a magnificently ornate room with a high vaulted ceiling, an ancient and enormous crystal chandelier and incidental sculptures of laughing Greek gods in every nook and cranny.

"Not to be indiscreet, Luke," Noëlle said, wending through the aggressively avant-garde crowd, "but you look awful."

I touched my bruised cheek and shrugged. "Just got back from Afghanistan," I lied. "Had a little run-in with a mullah's bodyguards."

"Not good." She tut-tutted and nodded toward my artist's portfolio. "You got some scary photos to show us?"

"I'm afraid this is business, not pleasure. Séverine wanted to make a few last-minute changes, so I brought some of her sketches over."

"I didn't know she worked from sketches."

"No, we all just make it up out of thin air, don't we?" I winked.

Noëlle nodded knowingly, as if I had just shared a confidence about Séverine. She then introduced herself to Giselle, instantly appraised and dismissed Giselle's pantsuit with a look, and told us to have some champagne before we went backstage. Instead of offering us the glasses she was carrying, however, she took them across the lobby, to a couple of women wearing matching neon pink tuxedos with absurdly large turquoise-checkered bow-ties.

Relieved that we had jumped this first hurdle without difficulty, I led Giselle to the bar at the corner of the lobby. The foyer around the outside of the main hall was alive with people in studiously outrageous and revealing attire, and as we weaved through the fops and poseurs, I leaned into Giselle and whispered, "Any sign of the Count?"

"Not yet."

"Take a glass of champagne, but don't drink any. Try to look natural, and keep your wits about you."

"*Oui, mon colonel*," she said, giving me a mock salute and then rubbing my arm to show that she was only joking.

"And don't be so familiar," I snapped. "Remember, I'm Séverine's boyfriend."

"I'm not the one who has trouble remembering that."

We ordered champagne, and I made small talk with the bartender, Thibault, whom I knew from other fashion functions. We chatted about the track-and-field championships that were taking place in Paris that week, while Giselle and I casually looked for the Count. I had seen Dumesnil only once before, as he'd shot at me through the rain, so I was not entirely certain that I would recognize him. I suspected he would be hard to miss, however—a septuagenarian Nazi with a big black briefcase in a sea of trendy youth.

After several minutes of empty sports patter and no sign of our Count, I touched Giselle's arm and nodded toward the main hall. It was a quarter till eleven when we left our drinks on the bar and strolled as casually as possible into the theater.

The Opéra-Comique is designed as a proscenium, with most of the seats on the main floor and two levels of balconies up above. The facades of the balconies are unbelievably rococo, crammed with tiny carved figures acting out violent scenes from ancient myths. The dominant colors are saturated red and gold, the colors of blood and money: a curiously ironic setting for light operettas.

Early 1960s Phil Spector tunes were playing on the house sound system—bubblegum pop songs by the likes of the Ronettes and the Chiffons—and Spector's Wall of Sound production suited the baroque pretensions of the hall remarkably well. For the fashion show, a black plasticene runway had been laid over the orchestra pit. The runway extended halfway up the theater's main aisle, so that the models would strut out from the wings of the stage, onto the stage itself, and then walk directly over the pit and into the main aisle. There, they would pass within a couple of feet of the audience. There were probably five hundred people already in the theater, fashion reporters and boutique buyers and quasi-celebrities, standing in the aisles in groups or sitting in the best seats next to the runway, comparing notes.

There was still no sign of the Count. I gave Giselle a worried look.

She shrugged. "I said eleven o'clock. He still has time."

I decided that we should go to one of the upper levels to get a better view of the crowd, so we retraced our steps to the lobby and found stairs leading up. No one at all was on the second level. We went into an empty balcony stage left. It was just a few minutes till eleven.

An announcement came over the loudspeakers inviting the audience to take their seats for the spectacle, and a chattering mob of people quickly filed in and filled up the area surrounding the runway. The Count did not seem to be among them. The house lights dimmed, and spotlights tinged red, purple and yellow played across the stage.

The early sixties girl-group music got louder, and the first model flounced onstage, to the accompaniment of an unseen emcee, who described her outfit. A parade of gorgeous, half-dressed women then followed, modeling Fendi's new fashions, and it was no longer possible to pick individuals out of the darkened theater. I looked at Giselle, who threw up her hands, and then we spent a few indecisive moments just watching the show.

Though Fendi is a relatively conservative design house, even conservative designers rarely button, zip or wrap their clothes in proper fashion around the models: a perfectly restrained blouse that your mother might wear to a civic function is allowed to hang off a model's shoulders, unbuttoned, exposing her breasts; or an ankle-length skirt will have only the uppermost button closed, letting the model walk right out of it with every other step. See-through blouses are never coupled with bras. In this particular show, every other model was wearing a hat, and despite my anxiety over the Count, I took a few seconds to appraise Séverine's handiwork.

There were black candlewick-yarn bonnets, trilby hats with gaudy ribbons, peaked mink caps streaked with sage dye, and a cloche with peacock feathers draped from the left ear. There was a mohair fedora, a hat made entirely of twigs and branches (like a hipper-than-thou crown of thorns) and even a green top hat with red leather ear flaps. Séverine had outdone herself.

"Look, over there!"

Giselle grabbed my arm and pointed to the other side of the theater. The figure of a man in a long, cape-like coat was entering the main floor through a side entrance. A second man, wearing an identical cape-like coat, followed him, and they stood for a few moments just inside the theater, looking around. They bent close to each other, and I could see in the half-light that the first man was carrying a briefcase. My heart beat faster and my palms sweat—half a million euros in cash, looking for us!

"Let's go," I said.

We left the balcony and walked quickly back to the second level foyer. I was limping rather badly, and Giselle practically pulled me down the stairs to the lobby, until I stopped her and motioned with my free hand that she should calm down and take it easy—the money was waiting for us, everything was fine. We needn't call attention to ourselves now. We entered the theater through the main door and stood for a moment at the very back of the hall, blinking hard to make our eyes adjust once again to the darkness.

Giselle tugged at the sleeve of my sports jacket. "Coming toward us," she hissed.

Count Dumesnil and his man were about halfway down the auditorium, and they had begun making their way toward the back of the hall along the side aisle. They had obviously seen us. I looked left and right: there was no one at all within twenty rows of the back of the theater.

I motioned for Giselle to take a seat in the back row. We could all sit down quietly, swap the two carrying cases below the level of the seats, and then get up and leave the theater. No one would see, no one would care.

We sat down exactly in the middle of the last row. I took a seat nearer the side aisle—nearer the Count—with Giselle on my right. The portfolio with the painting in it was on my left, ready for the swap. A giddy elation swelled inside me, and for the first time in two days I felt no pain.

The Count reached our row as "Be My Little Baby" came blasting over the sound system, and it was only then, much too late, that my instincts finally warned me that something was wrong. My gut, of course, was angry that I had come to the Opéra-Comique at all, but sheer self-preservation finally made it sound the alarm. My elation turned to nausea, and I felt a sinking low pressure, the kind of panic that makes pigs chase their tails before a tornado touches down.

"Something's wrong," I whispered to Giselle.

"Relax, nothing's wrong."

I broke into a cold sweat. I couldn't breathe. The Count came closer.

"Something's wrong."

Dumesnil stepped into our row, and the man with him followed, shuffling sideways between the seats. The Count held the briefcase out in front of him, half a million euros just a few feet from my grasp. Then I saw, out of the corner of my eye, coming quickly up the main aisle toward us, a man I recognized instantly even in the murky light of the dim theater—it was the buttery blonde man who had followed us!

"*Merde*," I said. "It's a set-up."

I jumped up and leaped over the row of seats in front of me. The artist's portfolio banged off of the armrests and hit me under the chin, and my bad knee buckled when I hit the floor. I fell awkwardly against the seats, scrambled to my feet and fell again. I evaded the Count with a duck and a scamper and felt the buttery blonde man closing from the other direction.

I crawled quickly to the side aisle, where I stood up and punched the Count's manservant in the stomach. He doubled over, and I scurried past him, out the side exit of the main theater and into a brightly lit hallway—but what awaited me there made my heart leap into my throat.

Half a dozen uniformed police officers stared at me in surprise and then quickly reached for their weapons. I froze for only an instant, and in that instant everything became clear: standing behind the policemen in an impeccably tailored three-piece suit was Joseph Danton, Impressionist Curator of the Orsay Museum. He froze for that instant just as I did, and our eyes locked.

"*La vache!*"

I threw myself back into the theater, where the darkness

momentarily blinded me again. I held the hallway door closed behind me, while the policemen pulled on it and shouted from outside. Something brushed against me—the Count!—and I realized that the buttery blonde man was holding the Count's arm, trying to get the briefcase full of money, and the Count's manservant was thrashing at the two of them.

Suddenly, Giselle vaulted into the aisle and legwhipped the buttery blonde to the ground, and the Count fell on top of him. The Count's servant hurtled off-balance toward me, and I ran down the aisle toward the stage. When I let go of the hall door, the police flung it open, and the Count's servant collided with the first policeman through the door. The aisle was now littered with squirming bodies in agonized positions.

The confusion afforded me only a moment's head start, and I used it to stagger to the front of the auditorium, toward the fly curtain at stage right. The fashion show was proceeding apace—the commotion on the side aisle wasn't yet loud or violent enough to draw attention away from the swirling colored spotlights and beautiful models and blaring music.

I pulled myself onto the side of the stage, away from the spotlights. I slithered under the curtain and dragged the portfolio behind me, and I found myself crawling between a paint trolley and a rack of black-hooded horizon lights. I stood up, threaded my way around some wooden set pieces, and made it to the models' dressing area. The Supremes' "Where Did Our Love Go" pleaded from the house loud speakers.

This entire wing of the theater, and the whole of the backstage, had been transformed into a brightly lit beauty salon, where models were frantically stripping out of outfits, draping themselves in new outfits, having their make-up re-touched and getting their hair plastered with fresh coats of lacquer. People were speaking all at once in a garble of mutually unintelligible commands, which were largely drowned out by the stage music anyway.

Lanky women wearing nothing but thong underwear were looking at their own asses in floor-length mirrors, assistants were running hither and thither with large but unidentifiable fashion accessories, and quite a few men and women with no apparent purpose, dressed in tailored jeans and designer t-shirts, were standing around staring into space as if stoned. I quickly picked Séverine out of the frenetic crowd: she was standing behind a model at a make-up table, adjusting the model's hat.

I had no clear ideas as I made my way toward her—I only knew that I couldn't outrun the police, that I had to get rid of the painting, and I had precious little time. I took the canvas out of the portfolio and left the portfolio leaning against a set piece. There was so much chaos backstage that no one paid the least attention to me, except the *coiffeur* whose foot I stepped on. He yelled "watch it," and smacked my shoulder with a round hairbrush, but went immediately back to tending his model's hair.

By the time I reached Séverine, I had decided that I would leave the painting with her—she could hide it in the make-up table while I led the police on a wild-goose chase, during which I hoped that the painting could be spirited out of the theater before the net closed entirely around us. Exactly how I hoped this would be done remains a mystery to this moment, but Séverine had always come through for me in the past, and she was now my last hope.

"Séverine!" I yelled. I grabbed her by the shoulder and spun her toward me. She reflexively threw her hands up to protect herself.

"Luke? What on earth—?"

When she saw the canvas in my hands and the bruise on my cheek, her surprise quickly turned to shock and fury.

"WHAT are you doing here?" This was a bitter accusation, and it was clear from the look on her face that she would not help me, but desperation had already trumped what little sense I had left.

"You've gotta hide this," I said. I thrust the painting toward her and looked over my shoulder for signs of pursuit. The cops had not appeared backstage, but they would be on me any second. "Please. Hide it anywhere. We've gotta get it out of the theater."

"Are you out of your mind?" She was so angry that she literally spit as she spoke. "Get out of here!"

"I'm *trying* to." I glanced over my shoulder again. "Please! Just hide it behind the mirrors or something when the cops come, then take it out of the theater when they chase me!"

"Cops?!"

There was no time left. I pushed the canvas into her arms and bolted toward the other side of the stage. Just then, two policemen appeared stage right, paused a moment, spotted me, then hustled through the rabble of stylists and naked models toward me.

Amazingly, the show was still going on. Runway models are so glazed as they strut into the spotlights that nothing fazes them, and the outre chic audiences are so nihilistic that even their own deaths might not shake their cool. "Da Doo Ron Ron" came over the loudspeakers, and I nearly bowled over a six-foot tall redhead in a vole-trimmed loden coat as I fled. The redhead said, "Hey!" but then it was her time to hit the catwalk, and she parted the curtains and flounced onstage.

I reached extreme stage left and poked my head around the fly curtain so that I could see the gallery. I was some distance away from the runway. I jumped down into the side aisle, gritting my teeth as I landed but limping on. I was now on the opposite side of the theater from where the chase had started, and I hobbled up toward the side exits.

I heard the police leaping off the stage behind me. I made it only fifteen rows up before they caught me, and I flung my hands in the air and leaned against an aisle seat, in a sign of surrender.

The first cop slammed into me anyway, so violently that I fell over the seat, pinning my arm against the armrest. The pain in my wrist as I toppled over was actually something of a relief, a momentary distraction from my tormented knee. The policeman pulled my head up by my hair, put me in an entirely unnecessary headlock, and then dragged me upright into the aisle. The second cop frisked me while the first one tightened his grip around my neck and the oxygen to my brain slowed. I couldn't breathe at all. My neck throbbed. I could feel my face turning red. When they were finally satisfied that I was unarmed, they wrenched my right arm behind my back to cuff me.

It was then, as the first policeman fumbled with his handcuffs, as my face began to swell with uncirculating blood, that I looked up toward the stage. On the runway, a model was swaggering toward the audience with the usual high-crossover steps, violently swaying her hips and looking down her nose with typical fuck-you attitude. She wore a silver floor-length dress with gray flower prints, and a chinchilla half-coat over it; but what caught your eye was not the high bodice of the dress or the angular cut of the coat—it was her hat.

The model was wearing an absurdly high, intensely colorful cone on top of her head. Though you couldn't tell from a distance what material the hat was made of, and though the emcee failed to describe it, I could tell all the way from the side of the theater that it was fashioned from century-old canvas and featured a pixilated scene of the Seine at Herblay. Séverine had turned the painting into a hat, and it was walking down the runway.

The policeman behind me finally got a solid grip on his handcuffs, locked my wrists behind my back, and released my head. As I choked air back into my lungs, I saw Joseph Danton run down the main aisle, leap onto the runway and snatch the hat off of the panicked model's head.

Séverine appeared stage right, her head peeking through an opening in the curtains. She saw Danton accosting the model. She looked into the audience and saw Giselle in handcuffs across the auditorium. Finally, she found me, bent awkwardly between two policemen, gasping for breath. She looked into my eyes for a long moment, then snapped the curtains closed and disappeared.

15

C'est la Vie

There are many lessons I could learn from this episode, if I were in a learning mood: lessons about the wages of crime, or about the wrath of women scorned, or even the simple wisdom of minding your own business. Mostly, though, I prefer to avoid the potentially edifying aspects of the tale and concentrate on my own bewildering stupidity.

Because I held art in such low regard, it never occurred to me that a man like Joseph Danton (after all, the curator of the most important collection of Impressionist art in the world) might be so well-connected that he could put me and my friends under police surveillance with a single phone call. I had considered him little more than a docent, a useful but inconsequential encyclopedia, and I had forgotten the elemental fact that, where there are high concentrations of money, there are always high concentrations of power.

The Orsay collection is worth hundreds of millions of dollars and unlike in America, where the arts are viewed with suspicion, in France the cultural officials actually acquire respect and influence through their positions. The fact that a man in Danton's position had agreed to meet with me at the drop of a hat should have been my first warning to stay away from the Luce, and the idea that Danton would be so unsophisticated as to accept my story about the Chechnyan black market at face value was absurd. I might just as well have told Danton directly that I had the stolen painting and wanted a ransom for it, just to save time; but underestimating Danton was only the first of many such critical mistakes.

I had also underestimated Séverine—or, to be more precise, I had taken her so much for granted that I had forgotten that she could turn against me. How I convinced myself so blithely to accompany Giselle on a black market errand to Séverine's fashion show I'm still not sure, and why I would then ask Séverine to help me hide a stolen masterpiece, with the police breathing down my neck, is a mystery. I suppose I could blame love—*l'amour est aveugle*, as some idiot poet once said—and I had fallen blindly in love with Giselle, but that was hardly a satisfactory explanation for everything that had happened.

Discounting love, then, my own behavior remained as unanswerable to me as the Sphinx's riddle. I couldn't say why I had been so vulnerable to Giselle's stupendous crisis. But then one day, as I was taking photographs of UNICEF workers in Burundi (part of my work-release program), I realized what had happened, why I had done what I'd done, and where the whole thing had gone wrong in the first place.

I was a victim of my own worst habits: my hubris, my tendency to live life vicariously, and the certainty that comes from accurately observing the foibles of others. As a war photographer, I had seen so many things go wrong in so many ways for so many other people that I thought I understood why they went wrong. I thought I understood the patterns of mistakes people make, and to a certain degree I was right—how else could I reproduce their mistakes with such flawless accuracy, if I had not observed them so well?

Petty thieves in petty markets, dime-store revolutionaries with dreams of conquest, religious fanatics uncompromisingly convinced of their ideals—all are victims of their own certainty, of seeing the mote in someone else's eye while missing the beam in their own. My luck, the thing that had always kept me out of trouble in the past, had worked only because I had no vain ambitions, no desire to impose my will on the chaos of life. I had only ever wanted to record the chaos, to expose the vagaries of conflict and the brutality of power, but I had never directly tried to change anything, gain anything, or stop anyone from doing anything before. I had always been a part of the confusion, so in tune with the riptides of turmoil that I could ride them safely out to calm waters, while others, who fought against the current, were sucked down and drowned in the undertow. The moment I wanted anything from the turmoil, I was sucked under like everyone else, and I made exactly the same errors and got into exactly the same trouble.

To this extent, then, I suppose I did learn a lesson: that my proper role in the world is as a witness, a recorder, a transmitter of the images of man's inhumanity to man. I have a knack for knowing what the story is and where, and with my camera, I can tell that story and I can move others in the telling. As an actor, though, as someone who wants to be part of the story, I'm just as selfish, amoral and incompetent as everyone else, and I vowed, after my involvement with Maximilien Luce, that I would follow in his footsteps. I would simply make a record of my observations, without attempting to assign value to them. If other people wanted to, they could try to earn a buck by stealing my work a hundred years after I was dead, or they could forget about me altogether, which would be more likely.

Value, I now believe, is an incomprehensibly intricate maze, a labyrinth that only the most arrogant among us—politicians, critics, *sommeliers*—can even pretend to navigate. The pretense of assigning definite values can only lead to dissatisfaction or violence, and the values you assign will probably change anyway. But I might be wrong about that.

* * * * *

The person who benefited most from our capture and arrest was not Joseph Danton, though the French press made him into a national hero; it was Benoît, who would be dead now if the police had not raided the *Mirabelle* on the same night they arrested me and Giselle. Between his gunshot wound (which turned out to be no trifling matter in itself) and the infection he had contracted from exposing the wound to the toxic waters of the Seine, Benoît was fast approaching grim death when special agents boarded the boat. They found him languishing below decks on a cot, shivering and unconscious, his skin a vegetal color approaching eggplant. They rushed him to the hospital, where he was kept for two weeks on intravenous fluids and antibiotics.

They charged Benoît with transporting stolen art, a crime with a maximum penalty of four years in prison, but Giselle testified that he had acted unwittingly, as a dupe, and the authorities had recorded no cell phone conversations featuring Benoît, because Benoît had never used a cell phone. Since he was not caught with the painting, there was no clear evidence documenting his participation, nothing incriminating enough to convict him, and he got off scot free. The black market thugs he and Regnault were holding aboard the *Mirabelle* refused to press charges, fearing, I suppose, that we would swear out charges against them and we would all end up in the same cell block. So the black market thugs went free and we were never made to answer for beating them and holding them hostage, and they were never punished for beating me senseless, twice—that, I guess, is the reward of honor among thieves.

Police found a quarter of a million euros' worth of diamonds floating in a black metal tube below Regnault's *péniche*, but since they could find no connection between them and any known crime, they could not charge Regnault with anything. It is not illegal, after all, to have a small fortune in diamonds floating in a tube in the river, though it's a sure bet that Regnault will be watched from now on, and his days of trafficking anything but coal up and down the Seine are over.

Séverine remained astonishingly above the fray, refusing to testify against any of us. She claimed that the first time she had ever heard about the painting was that night at the Opéra-Comique, and that she had turned the canvas into a fashion accessory to spite me for trying to involve her in something illegal. Her revenge made her a *cause célèbre* in the fashion world, and she was featured in magazine articles through the rest of the summer, next to photographs of the unfortunate runway model with the priceless painting on her head.

The Count suffered most. The authorities were only tracking him for his interest in illegally buying the Luce painting, which would have been bad enough; but when Giselle helped Interpol find the rest of his stolen art cache, which he had hidden in an old bomb shelter near his castle, his family's history as Vichy collaborators and his own secret life as an illegal art collector came out. In good Nazi fashion, the Count took a cyanide capsule in prison, and his estate now belongs to the Republic of France. The Count's servants, like most subordinate collaborators of the past, were deemed clueless unfortunates just following orders, and they all got light sentences, which were promptly suspended.

Giselle was charged with possessing stolen art, conspiracy to sell stolen art, and, in a gross indignity that was nevertheless true, with stealing the art that was stolen in the first place. In a plea bargain, involving the information that led to the recovery of the Count's other stolen artifacts, she managed to get off easy, with a five year suspended sentence. Her business and the reputation attached to it are ruined, but she now as plenty of time on her hands to decide what to do with her life, and she is no longer burdened with the moral and aesthetic quandaries of evaluating other people's treasures. She still talks about running away to a tropical island somewhere where no one knows us, so that we can start life over. At this point, I'm afraid to point out to her that "starting life over" is one of Jean-Jacques Rousseau's least persuasive fables.

Manon's participation warranted no prosecution, and she still laughs at the whole sordid episode and all of our vain pretensions. She was disappointed that she received no money from the caper, but she's happy with Giselle's BMW, which she kept, and she has adopted the Happy Elephant as her new family, and the Happy Elephant has adopted her. She can often be found there in the evenings, studying her school books or sitting curled in the corner with a glass of cassis and a Boris Vian novel or a play by Molière.

As for me: normally, as an American convicted of embezzling French art on French soil, I would have been obliged to serve my prison sentence and then been deported to the United States, my privilege of returning to France revoked forever. But in this case, I had an unlikely ally who pulled some strings on my behalf: Joseph Danton.

After my visit to the Orsay Museum, Danton had not only alerted the police and Interpol about me—he'd also familiarized himself with my work through on-line databases and newspaper archives, and he was impressed with the sympathy that my photographs often showed toward the suffering and dispossessed. Danton's grandparents had emigrated to France from the Congo, and his family had suffered in the atrocities committed there by Belgium's King Leopold. He maintained active interests in European aid work in sub-Saharan Africa, and he was even on the board of directors of several charity organizations with African ties. He immediately saw that I could be useful in publicizing his favorite causes, and he applied his weight with the French authorities to cut me a plea bargain: a two-year suspended sentence and the ability to continue to live in France, in exchange for working at subsistence wages for Danton's African projects during the two years of my sentence. It was a uniquely French solution, possible only under the arcane Napoleonic code, one in which the exact letter of the law could be superseded for an execution of justice more poetic in concept and more interesting to talk about than the dusty disinterest of written ordinances.

I had tried to sell a painting by Maximilien Luce in order to acquire a private fortune. I ended the affair by trying to help Danton convince rich people to share their fortunes with the poor. Life is funny.

* * * * *

On a chilly October evening, I walked down the five flights from my apartment to the street. It was just after seven o'clock, but the sun had already set—the days were getting shorter and grayer, and people were bundled in early winter clothing. The Marais was bustling as usual, and the pedestrians bumped and jostled one another on the narrow sidewalks. A shivering old Italian man was cranking the handle of an ancient calliope on the corner of rue du Pas de la Mule and rue des Tournelles—the circus music tootled pleasantly into the autumn air—and I was pleased by this typical Parisian absurdity. I stopped and listened for a few moments, put a euro coin into the man's basket, and then went around the corner to the fruit market.

"*Salut*, Luke," Etienne said from inside the market. He had already scuttled his sidewalk displays for the night and was sitting in a chair by the door, next to a little space heater. Most of his fruit was coming from Spain and Portugal now, since the

French season had passed. I bought a mealy-looking apricot. "I haven't seen your name in the paper for a while."

"No," I said, "I think I'm done being in the news. I'll stick to covering it." I told Etienne about the show of my photographs that Danton had arranged at the Luxembourg Gardens. "You should go see it."

"If I'm ever in that neighborhood, I will," said Etienne. "But sub-Saharan Africa—that doesn't interest me so much. Why don't you go to Algeria? It's a beautiful country, beautiful to photograph. I have relatives you could stay with."

I told him I'd think about it. I wished him a good evening and headed down rue des Tournelles, eating my apricot.

When I arrived at the Happy Elephant, Benoît was already there, sitting on a stool at the bar in his green City of Paris coveralls. Giselle sat next to him, perusing some colorful travel brochures. Manon reclined in an easy chair at the back of the room, her feet up on a coffee table, her nose in a thick book. Jean-Pierre was standing behind the bar, smoking a Gitane.

"It's still the most beautiful thing in Paris," Benoît was saying. "The most beautiful thing in Europe."

"It almost killed you," Jean-Pierre said.

"All beautiful things are dangerous. It's one of the things that makes them beautiful."

Giselle stood up to greet me. She gave me a wet kiss on the mouth and a big hug. "Hey, baby," she whispered in my ear. "How are you?"

Since the crisis of the stolen painting had passed, Giselle had become considerably more predictable in her everyday behavior, but she had not returned to her old uptight ways. She laughed more, told stories with more panache and seemed to enjoy life more, even though the life that she had always known had vanished before her eyes and she was left at loose ends.

Séverine had correctly predicted that Giselle's upper-crust friends would ostracize her once news of her involvement with the Count broke, and Giselle spent many nights with me almost in a daze, trying to make sense of all that had happened. She told me stories about herself that she had previously kept secret—stories about the nasty internal conflicts of her family, stories about Manon, about her relationship with Tristan. She sometimes became maudlin and pathetic, but I loved the fact that she needed me and I loved that she told me so. She was now more open and forthcoming about everything in her life, and her old strength of will had not entirely deserted her: she was learning, slowly but surely, to combine her calculating resolve with a new vulnerability, in a way that I found irresistible.

She had not taken another job and had sold nearly every heirloom she owned just to sustain herself in the most meager way. She still had significant debts, as well, but she seemed lighter and freer, and I would even describe her as happy. Of course, it's possible that I'd describe her as happy just because I felt so happy with her, the more so since Manon had become part of my life. As a result of Giselle's fall from society circles, Giselle and Manon had finally become civil to one another, and I often invited them both out to dinner, where we all talked intimately and enjoyed ourselves, just as any family of art thieves might.

Giselle and I sat down at the bar. "Benoît will always be in love with the Seine," I said to Jean-Pierre, picking up the thread of their conversation. "He still believes in river goddesses."

"It's the source of all life in the city," Benoît said. "And if you think that's a laughing matter, then you've got a funny sense of humor."

I ordered an armagnac. Jean-Pierre motioned for me to

slide down the bar with him, and I followed him until we could speak just out of earshot of the others. As he poured my drink, he said, "Séverine gave me a message for you today."

"Really?" Séverine had refused to speak with any of us except Jean-Pierre since the night of our arrest. Even Jean-Pierre had had to beg her to resume their friendship, and as much as he had lobbied on our behalf, Jean-Pierre had not been able to convince Séverine to rejoin our little group. My own letters to her always came back unopened; and the one time Giselle had visited Séverine's shop, Séverine had thrown a hat rack at her. Séverine had simply not been able to stomach our brief collective moral collapse, and she was still disgusted by the idea of me and Giselle together: her feeling of betrayal ran deep. "What did she say?"

"She said you should go to hell."

I waited to see if he was serious. "Séverine went out of her way to tell you to tell me to go to hell? That's the message?"

He stubbed out his cigarette and lit another one, then squinted at me through the smoke. "It's better than nothing." Jean-Pierre shrugged, and we walked back down the bar.

Manon had taken the seat next to Benoît, and they were boisterously disputing something Giselle had said about Vietnam. Giselle held up her glossy travel brochures as evidence in her defense.

I sipped my drink. It was going to be just another Thursday at the Happy Elephant.